AGOD

&

THEOCEAN

A Modern American Fairy Tale

Robin Hubbard

Cover Design Anya Ciarametaro

AGOD & THEOCEAN

A Modern American Fairy Tale

Library of Congress Copyright © 2017 by Robin J Hubbard

Imprint: Ragged Robin

Printed in the United States of America

First Printing, 2017

ISBN 978-0-692-95588-8
0-692-95588-7

For Oliver, Lara, Ainsley and

Wesley

A fictive dream . . .

RJH

The American dream is a myth now, in a post-capitalist world.

Chapter 1

Ptarro just missed cherry's peak bloom. Oh, a few wind-whipped petals managed to hang on after the last rain, but with their blossoms mostly faded and magnificence in the past, he was disappointed.

He looked around. A confusing network of concrete and steel cut across the sky – everywhere it seemed to crisscross and complicate. Suspended from it hung more roadway and ramp and there, in amongst a post-modern maze of abandoned access, where drivers once sped at dizzying speed, Ptarro saw Cotteeman, 400-year-old Cotteeman, an apparition tucked in leeward space, gazing at a double-blossomed cherry tree, absorbed in prayer.

He managed a quick climb. Reaching the spot where cherry grew, he curled his toes tightly round a rail running the length of the road and turned for a closer look. Cherry was there . . . in full bloom . . . but Cotteeman was gone.

Well . . . what do you know?

Ptarro hopped off the expressway and, walking along the river's edge, turned to scale a hill that opposed the Patowmack. Something terrible had happened and Geela had sent for him straight away. He had arranged his arrival to coincide with cherry's peak bloom, hoping its periphery of flower and blush might mitigate, somehow lessen, any disturbing imagery he was about to see.

He sucked in a wet whistle and sighed . . . he had missed it.

Quiet here, but chaos up there, he said to his self, while indicating the general direction with his beak. *Geela . . . Geela, where are you?*

Geela was an American eagle and employed by Treasury. The agency engraved her face upon its money plates and her countenance bolstered the value of its reserve notes, vouchsafing trust and confidence in the government . . . she was imprimatur of national honor and pride. But, as Treasury printed notes further and further, exceeding any rational restraint, she felt overexposed and exploited and, realizing she represented money more rather than America itself, threatened to leave and return to the Wilderness League.

They argued. Capitalism was failing, she said, and if government continued to sell its food supplies and all its land and forests and minerals out from under its people, they'd revolt. Back and forth and round and round, but nothing could sway either side and in the end it was over . . . finished . . . and Treasury tossed her out . . . out into the streets.

When Ptarro found her she was holding a book, its pages turning on the wind, one way then another, sunshine illuminating their ink. Animated figures of little people spilled off its pages while rapidly shifting wind panned and defied the natural order of things. It was a magic book and she had kept it for years. She wanted to explain, to explain that which was written so Ptarro could know and tell the others, before it was too late.

She said to him, "Some things pass and some things last and once you understand this you understand me. It's my morality."

"You see this? It's America's Book of Deeds. You see that hole, the one burning through its pages?"

Ptarro had never seen anything like it but said, "Yes . . . yes I do."

With rage and indignation she said, "Flame lit through those pages when Treasury broadcast money seed and printed money so fast and loose that it grew on trees. Here, let me show you."

Geela tilted the book so Ptarro could see. It caught hold of a sunray and she told him a story while its pages performed.

"Many, many years ago Treasury scattered money seed and just like Jack's magic beans the plants grew tall and fast. Treasury trained their stalks, like bean poles, to stretch as high as the sky, circle the earth and reach as far away as China."

"There, the people picked and picked as fast as they could, and they were clever, Ptarro. They created a hybrid note and grafted it to American money."

"How?" Ptarro asked. "Like a botantist would? Graft one stalk to another for better yield?"

"Yes, and today their hybrid grows all across the land."

"But Geela, there are no pollinators in China," Ptarro protested. "They were all killed in toxic plumes. How do they *do it*? How do the money plants do *it*?"

Geela laughed and paused a minute to consider the raptor standing alongside her and amidst all the confusion swirling about decided she liked him.

She continued, "Indeed, a remedy was needed, so a brilliant finance minister, and one from agriculture, devised a scheme. They deputized panda bears—you know, the ones in China that get royal treatment—and let them conscript, from all the billions living in China, an army corps of worker bees."

"The elites there, Ptarro, the big shots, chose from this corps the most skilled among them and overnight those millions marched out into the fields with their harvest ladders on their backs, leaned into the trees, and went to work."

"Using that old art form prized above all others in China, calligraphy, they dusted the anthers and stigmas to and fro and back and forth and, with their brush strokes, mimicked bees."

"Every day, a billion or more scrambled into the groves and climbed and picked as fast as they could. It was a race, you see, a race to the finish. The Chinese wanted their place at the table . . . they wanted to eat meat too . . . just like the Americans did."

"And with this, Asia ascended, and you know the rest of the story," Geela said, slamming the book shut.

"Holy Agod," said Ptarro, "what an enormous effort."

"You see, globalists made a deal with the American people and promised cheap consumer goods in exchange for their jobs and personal wealth and with that," Geela snapped her wing tips, "their supper plates were snatched right out from under them."

Ptarro stepped back and tilted his head. He looked confused and so he wouldn't miss the point of the story, Geela continued, "For Agod's sake, Ptarro, the Chinese raised seafood in agricultural sewers and exported it back to us. This is the crap Americans have been fed."

"Oh," he said slowly as epiphany gradually crept, lighting up his face.

"Well," said Geela, "the new American aristocrats are coming to vanquish me to old New York. But first, a trip to Jekyll; I must ask the old American aristocrats what to do."

Chapter 2

Americans were imprisoned by an economic system controlled by global corporations and, like eager, panting dogs, trotted merrily along on the road to serfdom . . . until it all went to crap.

Only a few ate meat. Western dominions, with their mock and unlimited immigration, had made it easy for corporations to exploit government and invest in foreign labor and as the rich became richer and richer around the world, the American worker was abandoned by a government controlled by global elites.

In the near future, globalism failed and debt obfuscated America's future because, in order to keep up, government had mortgaged its prosperity. Indeed, the American standard of living had been arbitraged and Americans so loaned upon that they became serfs. But corporations, you had better believe, managed to keep their money and their profit too, for they had contrived to keep everything and pay no tax at all.

The country had declined and in a post-capitalist world the dreams of so many were crushed. Chaos ensued, Americans lost possession of their culture and land. Crops failed, livestock perished and because global corporatists pushed policies of mass immigration and open borders, famine and starvation followed.

People were scarce, hard times had nearly finished them off. The West's version of capitalism had destroyed America and survivors abandoned technology and scattered into parkland tribes. All over North America boundaries were determined by ecosystems. The continent was a vast parkland of cooperating communities. They traded with one another—tent cities, tree huts, boat houses, beehives, under-the-ground shelters—and were modeled after a national park system; districts were arranged by task and were very democratic places.

With groundwater levels low, the earth dry and the sun dimmer everyday, Ptarro didn't quite know what to do but refused to accept that the fate that befell the government and economy would befall the land and all those who had managed to survive the onslaught of greedy and destructive human behavior.

A sense of duty roused in him. Animals and people had been competing with the whole world for a place in their own country . . . and it just didn't seem right. He considered recent events a worthy cause and a good fight. *This was my morality: cut out my heart, take my life, but don't eviscerate the land* and Ptarro promised Geela he would help restore the continent to health and swore to destroy the death makers of country, kith, and kin.

Chapter 3

Ptarro left Washington, and in a big hurry. He headed west and Geela, well, she flew south, towards the sandy beaches of Jekyll, the only place she knew to go.

The coastal plain he trudged along allowed for a fair view of the city. As the day advanced and he clomb higher and higher, he stopped to take the view. Below the roads leading in and out of the capital seemed to shrivel and shrink, their suburbs no longer sprawled but tightened, parting to extinction. He watched a monument spin out of control and drop, dramatically folding to its death. Everywhere he looked centuries of American legacy lay littering the streets. The country's tribute to power and glory had spilled o'er the land and, oh, he was very, very sick.

With America's history chucked, uptown and downtown, bridges and buildings, once new and promising, declined, then gone – only the Capitol remained intact. Everywhere debris piled high, and on one heap laid Geela's treasure, its sheets turning on the wind while miniature action of story animated above its pages.

Gone, sighed Ptarro. *She was holding it . . . trying to explain . . . what was she trying to tell me?*

Inside the manuscript, Ptarro had caught a glimpse of a banker's calendar and in it its accompanying schedule of unlimited war. Constant entanglements had made the rich richer and richer, but their hour of reckoning had come . . . and Geela's, too, of course.

Ptarro watched as an old woman weaved her way around it all. She was wearing a dress and straw hat and, with the help of a cane, bullied and pushed past the others. *Well, ain't she well-fed . . . and well-dressed,* thought Ptarro. She stopped a minute and looked about, straightened her glasses and, hooking her cane on her one free arm, hobbled over to a trash can tucked just inside a fancy gate leading to the lush interior of a nearby park.

Her ankles were large and from behind, her feet, the tiniest part of her body, appeared normal in size but just at the ankle a swell began and moving upwards, filled her all the way to where her elbows leaned into the bin.

Probably rich, thought Ptarro, *an old woman with money . . . I am sure of it . . . they're easy to spot.* She placed her cane to rest against the barrel.

Ptarro could hear the warmth inside the garden. The wind was soft and bird song accompanied the murmurings of those in the park. It was a starry day indeed.

Oh, my, Ptarro thought, *first the lone cherry gazer, and now this.*

People sat in sunlight and idly chatted while others ate from bags packed at home. A hedgerow of shrubs circled the grounds and from inside the bush sparrows chirped, singing praise and glory to the Sun Life. A breeze blew on easy sunshine and shook loose boughs that sent their lovely chorus windward. A gust of wind and tempo quickened . . . then leeward fell . . . bouncing and tumbling towards descending pitch.

Meanwhile, picnickers finished their snacks and began to toss the scraps and the old woman, with no particular odor but the face of an omnivore, bent and dug through the discarded wrappers and using her fists, like the chipmunk would, ravenously pushed food into her mouth but rather than store it in the jowls like the chipmunk would, she shoved it straight down to the belly and, finishing off with a one-two punch, really packed it in. When she was done she dropped her fists and brushed them off on her skirt. No one seemed to notice.

She quit the park and wandered back the way she came, passing through a square along the way. At its edge a sparkle, a glint off a shaft of sunlit beam, caught her eye and she went in for a closer look. She saw Geela's book. Its pages shone and the old lady with the swollen body picked it up, stuffed it in her satchel and continued on her way.

From a precipice Ptarro cried out, and swooned. Rocking heel to toe, back and forth, revulsion swept him, and fear climbed in. It tore at his heart and his gut sank with its weight. When fear ascended and seized his jaw, it ached so that he could not cry—a pool of poison threatened and slopped its slimy taste—his organs stalled, and he slumped to the ground. When violent sobs shook loose his more tremulous cries, his life force tripped and, oh, he was very, very sick.

Above it all, beyond the Patowmack, a tattered gull flew over the ruin. Struggling and hooked and entangled with string, its flight erratic and distressed, Ptarro watched as its one free wing managed to guide it through a clear blue sky.

His screams returned and, beseeching, he cried out, *Oh, Agod, my sunlight is dim and my water is low . . . cut out my heart, my life . . . gut me. Oh, Agod, I beg you, take away my suffering, evacuate my fear . . . protect me from anxiety.*

Again fear descended but this time libido stirred and brought him back around. Bile floated his pink, hairy tongue . . . an emetic discharged and expelled dark fear.

Ptarro rejected what his heart knew, what his head knew . . . he wanted none of it. *Expel dark fear or the devil will take you, isn't that what Wreda would say?* His father might die or his mother, but certainly he could trick death . . . couldn't he?

All around him people were sick and trying hard to stay alive. Their mothers and fathers were gone, a way of life passed by and . . . *Yes, I'm afraid. My mother and father are dead, and there's no one to take their place.* He was so low . . . so low . . . how will it all end?

Death inhered in life. Ptarro knew this, and knew his history too. The Roman Empire fell, but somehow Italy survived; England's reach retreated, yet London remained the finance capital of the world and while France thumbed its nose at most everyone, America, oh, America, all of it, thank Agod, retained its primordial glory . . . its land, its wilderness, and its people too.

He repudiated fear. An old and fearless bird, Ptarro is a raptor who cannot fly.

Chapter 4

Nearby, a radio blasted the noontime news. The talking heads were at it again, but lately . . . somehow . . . they were quieter. *Subdued by humility perhaps?*

Maybe. After all, Washington was in chaos, ruined, and most survivors had scattered into parkland tribes. Oh, once upon a time the broadcasters talked, talked-talked, talked-talked all day long and at the end of the week they postured and posed and hosted yet more talk, talk-talk, talk-talk about what they had talked, talked-talked, talked-talked about all week long. *Yuck.* For decades Americans had bent a collective mind to their cerebrally trivialized gymnastics, but no more; people had figured it out and could think for themselves. Media was irrelevant, thank Agod, their great period of persuasion in the past. Their daily messaging had been the same for so long and, as nothing really ever changed, most rejected their constant harangue, and pursued Another Way.

Like starlings in spontaneous ascent, survivors flocked and headed for the parklands. Oh, media tried hard to tell people what to do, what to think, what to worship and how to do it, and was sure people would be persuaded, but in the end, people could not be trained to think what they were told. Media had bet wrong and with their mental whirl all too bizarre and their headlines reflecting moralities that did not endure, like little birds in an autumnal preparation, people pursued Another Way because, by now, the American Dream was a myth.

Those refusing to leave watched as their creature comforts slowly faded and dissolved and while the great, modern epoch, with its regents and donors and sycophantic surrogates and darlings of broadcast, slid towards redundancy, the big shots lost the imperium. What had it profited the elites to gain the whole world and lose Agod in the process?

Media darlings, Ptarro thought, *sparkling, startled, media darlings . . . damn.*

Ptarro preferred Another Way, the parkland way and he was thankful because encoded in his DNA, like that of many others, was the wisdom that showed him how to live well and make good sound judgements and like him, so many had awakened.

Americans were constipated with greed. Was it delicious? Contaminated and poisoned, they couldn't poop and when their country declined, and a new world order followed, their dreams and collective myths crashed down, down, down. In the ensuing chaos, most were stripped of their culture and land and when crops failed and livestock perished, famine and starvation followed. All across the land people lamented and lost.

Chapter 5

In the beginning, Agod, who was both mother and father, created Geela and eagle was born. Geela was part of the Wilderness League and it existed long before America was ever dreamed up.

The first League members were premonitory, prescient societies of birds and their gods extinct creatures. Guidance was sought from the spirits of Mohave chub and passenger pigeon, Carolina parakeet and Labrador duck, harelip sucker and heath hen, Palos Verde butterfly and black-footed ferret, and all the others who vanished long before these had.

Of course the League members were polytheists because, heck, so many among them were dead . . . vanquished forever. Their intermediaries, the ones who carried their prayers back and forth between the two worlds, ordinary reality and the divine, were creatures near extinction. After all, who was a better messenger than one slipping towards biological annihilation?

The land was like a dream. In summer birds congregated alongside cascading riverbeds to court and mate and breed and play. They gathered on the quiet, stiller marshes in the north and collected along the livelier coasts too. Summer's warm breeze carried their chatter and, while sun-soaked seed heads burst o'er the land, gay frolics and daily dips and lots of splashing was everyday way.

In the evening, fireflies spoke, their flashing light blinking optical code, lighting up their campsites with brilliant firework displays. Long and short flashes signaled a Morse Code-like alphabet, and the birds played at it like a game of charades. It was great fun, staying up late into the night, laughing, playing, guessing and posturing.

The flies were scouts and loved to play with the birds and their guests. Each summer they visited and flashed reconnaissance and as the epics passed their messages evolved to include human movement and migration patterns. People were swarming all o'er the place, their ascent impacted all, and changes in water flow and rainfall and fractures and scars tempered and altered the land, affecting everything.

White pelican attended the parties. They brought oranges and apples, peaches and plums, and grapes and berries and nuts collected from all over the land. Some even carried wine and, tilting their heads, with a generous pour, served it straight from flapping-loose neck pouches for those eager to imbibe.

Clipena was pelican's leader and there came a time when she began to warn that one day all this would be gone—so drink up and be merry—for the time will come when it will be much work to bring it all back and, soon enough, she and her pelicans were no longer celebrating at summertime parties but carrying supplies to the troops in the field of the Wilderness League.

Thus the League operated in order to better survive towards the end of the last modern epoch in America. Its members who were not yet extinct tracked natural resource levels around the continent, generating intelligence that allowed those who would listen a chance to anticipate things; a farmer might move and plant certain row crops farther north, for instance, or stay put and switch crops all together, planting seeds suited for a temperate clime in a previously cooler place.

Over time others joined the birds: insects and fish, mammals and people, anyone, really, who managed to survive, who looked ahead and made it through the onslaught of greedy and destructive human behavior. They had kept their heads down and practiced Another Way for decades, quietly, and together they made a difference.

Towards the end of the happy season a hush fell and silenced their songs and playful romps. Winter began its approach and its milk light muted gray the white bone of cold, inciting the northern skies.

An upward roar swept simultaneous ascent as innate homing instinct migrated flyways and skyways and collided with time. Millions took flight and, up on an equinox edge, embarked upon ridges of invisible wind and warm thermal drafts and, safely inside, were austral bound.

Winter stirred. Trees shuttered any lingering autumnal leaves and headed for bed. Some flew towards Blooming Flower, a popular destination in winter, though Aurora Australis gladly guided those venturing farther south, into its zone.

When spring returned Ephemeral's shroud dressed dormant fields and draped, like lace sheets, gossamer snow fall. Seed heads railed and awakened Agod's vernal wellspring. Hearkened, snow had movement now, here then gone. A luxuriant sun trailed a train of silk, one day after another across the mountains and valleys, and web spinners wove their raiment and completed yet another metamorphosis.

America's ascent brought changes to the land, with it massacres and surges in human migration. Oh, the first people had tried hard to take a stand but in the end retreated and hid best they could but after America's experiment with capitalism failed, the League reemerged seeking its rightful place, and some of the extraordinary ones were reborn.

Ptarro's god, Agod, yearned for a society of good stewardship to ensure survival of the earth, the animals and the people too. Agod must be restored to power. Agod was not at odds with nature but in harmony with it. Agod's realm was the Occident, all of it, its wilderness, its wildlife, and its people too. Those who had made it through, the good and smart among them, had figured it out: in order to ensure the survival of the land, it was necessary to cultivate an appreciation for everyday way, the Sun Life way. Agod must rule, not the corporatists, not the donors, not the trilateral commission, not the committee on foreign relations, not the OAS, not mock – Agod. So the Wilderness League embarked on journeys to save what was left of America: its people, its animals, and its wilderness too.

Revenge was part of the plan, because along with the culture and economy and never ending consumption and greed, the fat ducks had destroyed too much. A price had to be extracted so it would never, ever happen again, and the Wilderness League went to war with the remaining bad guys . . . particularly the overly acquisitive ones.

Can the League save the animals, the land, and those who embraced Another Way, the Sun Life, or was it too late? Had the experiment with globalism and the West's version of capitalism destroyed America forever, its land, its people, its culture, and its wildlife with its never ending consumption and greed?

Chapter 6

Back in her apartment the old woman took off her hat and placed it on a table that stood near the door. It was hot inside and a fan blew warm air around the room. She unfastened her dress and let it fall to the floor and, plopping her huge frame into a chair, sat down for a closer look at what she had found.

From across the room came a stir. Someone was sleeping on a day bed pushed against the wall, drawing deep, soundless respirations. She opened her eyes and, turning her head without lifting, asked with a very small voice, "Lithil, is that you? What's that in your hands? I can feel its power. I could feel it as soon as you entered the room. It clung to my breath and invaded my dreams."

Lithil held up a beautiful book and when she did its pages flew open. Playful scenes with tiny characters came alive, performing in fast forward and reverse motion; simultaneous whirls of color and action scrambled and blurred.

"Whoa," said Lithil, slamming the book shut. "What's this I've found? And on a rubbish heap?"

Occo was an ancient American woman with an old soul and ate just enough to move her rickety old body. She got around with a cane, just like Lithil did, and loved clothes. She was extraordinary looking, really, and very, very thin. Why, today, just around the house, she was wearing a black chemise over a long black smock, underneath a black slip was edged out in lace and high-top shoes and black hose topped off her look. All her garments were made of silk and while she was white-haired and stooped and looked like she could have walked out of a forest, she was dressed like a woman from Paris . . . an ancient woman from Paris.

Occo's shoes were dangling and hooked from feet that extended through a tangle of bed clothes. Her legs were long and veiled and well-manicured, yellow-painted toenails pushed past the tiny peeps in her pretty shoes. Through the sheer of her stockings brightly-polished, creamy sunflower points reached and scratched an itch. Near the bed was a bug box, and in it her current companion, a green June beetle. She had outlived her husband for so long she couldn't remember his name and when she walked, she walked very fast, even with a cane – still, she barely breathed. She drove a car, that is, when she could find one that worked – she had always owned a car, until the authorities outlawed driving. She had been born one hundred years before cars were built and was very disappointed when her car was taken from her . . . She had seen a lot.

When she was still ancient, Occo ran the entire distance across the state of Florida in one night. She ran past trees of gold and lady palms, purple queens and sky vines, trumpet creepers, silk trees, china berries and birds of paradise. It was no effort at all and as she ran she inhaled the smells of an exotic plant world and felt the humidity against her skin and like so many others understood why what seemed like the whole world had come with their capital and labor and built temples, and celebrated what Blooming Flower had to offer. Glamour, sun, orange trees, beaches, art deco, palms, bikinis – the place was hopping and filled with people in love with Blooming Flower and as she ran top to bottom, past, present, and future were revealed to her in abandoned, faded fun and in attempts to place the new inside the old.

She liked it and opened a shop in Miamia, in the way south of Blooming Flower. Day in and day out she clerked, meeting travelers from all over the world. Occo was in heaven. She swam in the sea before opening her shop, some days going directly to shop from sea. She may have looked unkempt, she liked to say, straight from sea to shop, but she felt refreshed and didn't care—she was so glad to be alive—plant wisdom and the wisdom from their roots had spoken to her when she ran through Florida that lovely, fateful night, and she never forgot it.

With the breeze from the window in her ear she rose like a queen from off the day bed and glided across the room. She took the book from Lithil's hands and looked closely at its pages, and all its animated characters. She recognized it. As urban sounds lifted from the street below and drifted through the open window she noted it was gorgeous and told Lithil it was an old illuminated manuscript from America's glory days and as long as the sun was shining and the wind gently blew, it would perform. But it needed to be opened slowly, one page at a time . . . or else . . . watch out . . . helter-skelter.

Occo knew well the terrible story of America's decline, and all the more sadly so, because she had seen so much.

Why hurry the story along, she thought.

Outside, a vestigial Washington murmured in warm sentient sound, but with a chattering, disconnected voice. Nearby, the people who were dining and drinking and laughing and visiting friends seemed oblivious in a place just as rich as Miamia but more reserved and subdued; a residual, quiet, brain-trust culture, not a crazy, wild, megacity culture like the one in Miamia – northern establishment money, not drug money from the southern Americas.

The people talking, distinguished and high-browed, dressed fairly casually but then the whole country dressed casually, too casually really. *Who wanted to look like an American anymore,* she mused. She sighed. *Once upon a time, Americans were admired all over the world – great arbiters of style. Oh well . . .*

Their glamour, the spell they had cast over spectators around the globe had dissolved with the rise of an insouciant nonchalance, when irreverence became vogue. Or was it something else?

She sucked in her breath and thought, *Oh, I don't know. Oh my Agod, what a godless, ungrateful place this country has become* . . . She sighed again.

They had roasted Bug Bites to snack on, and together with the green June beetle, who was only too glad to be companion of the day and not a tasty treat, the ladies sat down to watch the story of America. Occo showed Lithil how to properly open the book and together they watched it perform. The book was animated and had the power to see past, present, and future.

Occo knew she and Lithil metamorphosed in the story, but Lithil was a contemporary woman with a younger soul and not aware of this and needed to be shown. Somehow time stopped and, when it did, Occo opened the book and turned to her friend and they flew into the story as Greet Withe and Wreda Blord.

Geela said, "The two currencies were one, Ptarro. Before the hybrid process, each country had had its own specie but the rich wanted to be super rich and rule the world and one specie wouldn't do, didn't yield nearly enough, so central bankers repudiated gold and expanded the world's mock supply and, for a while, pulled it off – a monumental theft of global assets succeeded and the entire planet was securitized."

Treasury's program burst forth branches of busting green foliage, heavy with harvests belonging to future generations, and the trees yielded year-round. Gluttons stuffed themselves, binge eating more and more, always more and more than their fair share from off the world's offertory plate.

New castes of kings and queens were created. Workers and nurses, housekeepers and drones, the dispensable beings, burped out business cycles, and the seasons blurred. And while central banks manipulated the two currencies, allowing a new caste of kings and queens to steal the whole world out from under its people, only an occasional currency war could interrupt the binge.

But greed got in the way and the democratization of mock failed.

"Capitalism began in one of the oldest civilizations on earth," Geela shouted out as she flew off.

"And America bombed the crap out of that place – all gone to the devil because of greed and waste. The West's version of capitalism had far-surpassed anyone's wildest imagination. Why, the whole world was securitized, and everything in it. America was very greedy, and the Book of Deeds will show that."

Chapter 7

A man on a bicycle rode by. He was clinging tightly to its upright handlebars and pulling a two-wheeled cart behind him. It was stuffed with food supplies and he grimaced and struggled with the weight of it.

Automobile manufacturers had stopped building cars and domestic fuel stocks were largely depleted so the pace of life was slower now. Still, one could be in a furious hurry on a bicycle, and this one raced feverishly by.

He wore a jacket cut like the ones ball players had worn. The denim in the short garment was pinned with badges and medals. He kept his kinky hair long and worked it daily into white, tightly-woven braids. Like most people, those who had survived anyway, he had made the journey back to find what had been lost and once recovered held on tightly and remembered how to live. Star watchers gazed at ten-thousand-year-old time and wondered how it, so talented and vast, could travel backwards and forwards, stop and standstill, and still reach the earth. They were sure the past had not passed, but was here.

This one had been a boy scout. He looked a little crazy, particularly around the eyes, and Ptarro knew him.

Ampersand was, oh, maybe in his late fifties. An older guy, not really old, but older-looking—worn out—*heck, he's probably younger than me.* Thin skin slipped his prominent frame, his well-greased body worked hard and, although it was hot and humid, he looked rather dry.

Hunger hung his face. He was as a little boy, yes, the man was a little boy, but with a face like that could claim a hard life. Thin, lean and wiry, *he probably doesn't get enough to eat,* Ptarro thought. *Poor bugger, a ligature of letters. How did he get that name, I wonder?*

"Do you want a lift? I'm on my way to Dakota. Lots of hungry people there," Ampersand asked as he smiled and waved. A young adolescent sat in back, on top of the food pile, whistling. Walker was her name, Whistling Walker. She smiled and waved too.

People had nearly exterminated wildlife, and native people too, for that matter, more often than not for the sport of it, and many were massacred to extinction, but in Dakota today the whole thing had turned around.

Of all things, prairie dogs were now caring for Cold People, survivors who had dug in along the abandoned hydraulic fracturing sites in Dakota, seeking heat. Not so long ago farmers and ranchers had hated them – their lifestyles and landscaping techniques had simply been in the way of their progress. But in the end it was the frackers who damaged the Great Plains most of all, poisoning the groundwater and forcing people out and when the dogs returned home and reclaimed *la prairie*, extending their range back down towards Texas, they found Cold People living nearby.

Wind rustled grass stalks and rattled seed heads. In amongst stems taller than people, sun sang and birds did not quarrel. A wren in shadow, announced with a little song, before light soaked the land, the sunrise and greeted day with wholes and halves and clappered quarters, compounding simple meter.

Birds tweeted musical notes: one, two, then three beats and, pausing a moment, shrilly sang great praise to sun's life. The company was good, trilling *tat a tat tat tat* in *la prairie* and, gurgling, greeted dawn, the light . . . Agod's light . . . a day that would never come again.

Sun sang warmly now. A cincture of crickets wailed like sirens, insects stung staccato, cicadas swept random pattern and heat bugs beat pulse along a buzzing edge of random flight while sweet pollinators sounded sliding whistles of acoustics in the crest and troughs of grass, vibrating the inner ear of prairie dog. This was home.

Blowing softly and steadily, warm gusts wisped over crickets and chippering toads, cheeping and chirping, humming sweetly around wafting, winged flower scent. Out of range of birdsong, shouting sunflowers drilled and, snapping finger cymbals, their ratchets and dissonance chimed as triangles of wind squeaked and squealed and jingled their bells. Sunflowers got their power from the Sun Life and the intelligence in their roots and the melody in the nearby hollow burrows paused and listened for sunflower was conducting this conversation in the tall grass.

First fossil fuels were depleted then food crops withered and died; roles were reversed and animals managed people, that is, if people were to survive. There weren't many left, so why not? *Wildlife management? An oxymoronic phrase, if ever I heard one,* Geela had said, once upon a time. *But human management . . . now . . . that sounds about right. A charity cause, like native people helping the early arrivals from England or Spain . . . we should beware . . .*

A splinter group of remainers, Cold People lived near neglected drill shafts and huddled together, always shivering, always cold. They existed off crumbs, and most everything they needed for survival was gleaned from heaps of rubbish. The parklands were not for them − Cold People were junkyard junkies and preferred idle industrial sites abandoned by formerly enterprising folk. Caren Shilland was their advisor and wanted that they learn to live Another Way, but faced stubborn resistance.

Cold People built their shelters in prairie dog territory, not thinking the dogs would ever return. They used discarded tin and cardboard, anything they could find, really; nails were pulled from old boards and pounded straight again, then hammered back into wooden boxes arranged under plastic roofs. They sifted through refuse dumps for appliances, metals, plastics, asphalt, and wire and repurposed these items to furnish their shacks and their huts were heated by residual drafts of underground gases left behind in the abandoned fracking shafts.

Ampersand was a friend to them. He rode all over the country, trading scavenged junk for food. He was a great ally and scout.

"I could put you in my basket," shouted Ampersand. "I got to get to Middle River, though, fast and furious. Then north to Missouri, along the old trails that follow the Platte, on back to the prairie dog towns. There are a lot of hungry people there."

"Not goin' your way, but thanks anyway. Wishtonwish is waiting for me, up ahead in the Alleghenies at the big-rock meeting place." Ptarro gestured in the general direction with his beak.

"He and I will follow the Ohio to Middle River, then head south, to Arkansas. Got to get to Ozark anyway we can. It's where the ants live."

"All the way to the ant colony," Ptarro sighed. "It's quite a hike, and I can't fly no more," he said, lifting a mangled wing.

"Wishton?" Ampersand asked. "I know 'im. Give 'im a message would you?"

Wishtonwish's famous name was imitative of a prairie dog's cry and those who lived along the great meadow and in the river district easily recognized it.

He forced the foot brake and screeched to a halt. The little dog in the back fell off the pile and cried.

"Hey watch it, will ya?" Walker screamed. "Coulda broke my neck."

Ampersand looked a little annoyed with his hitchhiker. She was a difficult teenager.

"Tell 'im Duluth is a ghost town and at the straights the Mackinac Boat People of the Great Lakes are demanding a toll to cross the bridge . . . 'course they guarantee a safe crossing . . . but it ain't safe . . . still, people wanna get across. They're journeying north, to where the Happy People live in Sequoia. Chicago ain't much better 'cept them bankers there are still exchanging mock for things. Not so out in the parklands, I'm afraid."

"I'll tell him; can't blame them . . . for collecting a toll."

Government debt was high and America's trading partners demanded settlement in gold. The corporate elites knew the gold was gone, however, and had forced America to sell its food supplies, its land, its mineral rights and everything else of any value. The nation had no collateral left to secure lines of credit or guarantee its debt obligations. It had expropriated its citizens' wealth and mortgaged their futures way past a place in time where their children could hope . . . they had become perpetual serfs.

Widespread drought and failed capitalism destroyed the American economy and survivors scattered into parkland tribes and lived Another Way, and there they found enough and danced and celebrated life with awe, wonder, and amazement. They could poop, and weren't constipated. They ate only what was needed and were happy living the Sun Life way. Still others held onto grudges and wanted their old lives back.

"You don't look so good, 'tarro."

Ptarro was still lying on the ground, pulled his self up, and brushed off.

"Excuse me; just come from DC. Treasury fired Geela and they came for her so fast, there was no time to think and, to be honest, it depressed me."

Amp put his foot to the pedal and rode off. The little dog clamored back on the food pile and held onto her hat. They picked up speed and disappeared from sight and Whistling Walker waved until she could no longer see Ptarro.

He tried to put the weird scene in DC behind him. He looked west, towards Middle River, but remained deeply troubled. Most survivors from the east had headed in that direction, fleeing the chaos, and like him, had a lot on their minds.

Wishtonwish was just ahead, waiting at the big-rock meeting place. Somehow they'd get to the ant colony; they would walk, take boats, float, get there any way they could. But first, a few days to himself.

Chapter 8

Ptarro pushed ahead but without his wings didn't make good time. He was struggling. His good friend Wishtonwish was just ahead, waiting, at the big-rock meeting place so he gave it his best effort, but Ptarro was stuck in his body and it distressed him. He tried hard, but wasn't able to control his thoughts and they wandered back to the days he spent in Chesapeake where, a few years earlier, his whole life changed.

He had been standing there, on a hot patch and Wreda Blord was sitting in a shady spot, at the river's edge . . . her stout legs were dangling in its slow-moving current. He looked over at her—she was going on and on about the merits of the Maplewood campaign—but he wasn't really listening. His mind was distracted. He stood with his hands in his pockets and scratched the dry dust with his claws.

"You know, 'tarro, America ought to own its own food supplies. Globalism will fail . . . Geela likes to say . . . and in a big way. Allowing other countries to buy into our food supply, well, it was a lousy, bad idea and set a poor policy precedent."

He said nothing; smiling a little, Wreda tried to coax him around.

"The Chinese like to keep their food alive till just before cooking," she teased and, throwing her head back and laughing and craning just a little, looked to see if his sense of humor had returned.

Wreda likes to play with her prey, he mused, grudgingly to himself.

"And on top of that, they want their little girls back," she said, continuing to bait him.

"You know the ones they put on planes to fly away to the rich West all those years ago? Well, their population is aging and they want 'em back, to replace the ones who are dying. Can you believe it?"

She was trying real hard to censor herself, but she just couldn't manage it.

"America, matter-of-factly, said no, of course." And slapping her thigh, her laughter resumed and choking and snorting, she spit out, "Them Chinese don't want to encourage a nation of same-sexed couples."

He rolled his eyes and smirked. *Two spirits,* he thought, *Chinese two spirits,* but quickly dropped his head. He was still kicking the earth when chagrin's hot shame flushed o'er him, and melted him down.

"Somehow, I fell," he wailed. "I don't know how, dammit, but I fell. My toe nail tangled and I tripped or . . . oh, heck, I don't know . . . but I fell. And that clumsy tumble tore my wing feathers, dammit. Now I get around like a grounded grange chicken, walking and a-hop flying wherever I go."

Wreda swished her thick legs to and fro. Swirls of water spattered about her calves while a hopeful sparrow called out for courtship from deep inside the bush. She sighed. She'd seen a drone knock him out of that tree but didn't want to say, so she began talking of Vancouver, where she was needed in the fall. She chatted on and on about the trip and because she had just recently embarked on a physical fitness regime said she intended to run the entire distance there. At Huron she thought she'd stop and rest awhile then float across to the Canadian shore.

She sighed and heaved herself up from off the ground. Her bulky frame brushed against the shadbush bloom, dispersing its scent. A lovely fragrance followed her to where Ptarro stood.

She looked into his eyes and saw deep inside his raptor's brain and her stare drew a shadow that, somehow, retrieved his courage. "You're valuable, Ptarro, and Geela's got great plans. There are many journeys ahead and your service is needed. You can no longer fly so . . . buck up . . . adapt . . . learn to walk."

She watched him step back. He took in her words alright, but the shock creeping across his face betrayed his astonishment. Disbelief cast its pall and his ears, well, he just couldn't believe his ears.

Later he confided to Wishtonwish, "My Agod, she expected me to pick myself up and carry on."

"Journey west," she commanded. "The red ants need a leader."

And with that she was gone.

Daylight's aperture was narrower now, but the sun remained larger than life.

Chapter 9

Ptarro lie down to rest. He was trying to remember something that never happened . . . that he'd seen in a dream. Time stopped and he changed worlds. His wings worked again and he flew towards a place called Blooming Flower, a land where thousands of flamingoes lived. Along the way passenger pigeons darkened the sky and in numbers so great people could never, ever be a threat to them again. His dream filled with the rushing noise of their passage and they hailed him, for they had a message.

"The gone are gone, in the ground," the passengers said. "On your way to long ago, you'll see Greet Withe. She has climbed into the body of a plume bird and put on a breeding costume – and she wants revenge."

"Her feathers are luscious and she'll lure many men to a dense mangrove off the coast of Blooming Flower. She aims to kill them all, all them plume hunters. Gather together forces and help her."

The day the pink plumes were killed, all the birds died.

That day was still, the kind of still that sets up before stifling. The wind, barely audible, was hardly felt, and warm too. Trees stood unassailed and unapproached, stoic trees that belied the crazy fornication of their beginning. Their young leaflets lifted and gasped a deep breath, held it . . . and then . . .

Along the edge of the camp strangler vines, blood lilies and Spanish bayonets, dumb canes, fire spikes and thorns, bleeding hearts, crowns of thorns and snake plants bordered Greet's territory. She passed water and stayed long enough for other wild creatures to grow accustomed to her scent and, by its virtue, accustomed to her presence, and they existed untroubled and unthreatened in the shared space.

Dusk approached. Greet hosted a shooting party. She chose a camp under a dark wreath of tree where vulture kept a roost. Noisily, they flew in and out and on and off one tree limb then another, flapping loudly and snapping branches. For a long while the racket did not cease, then settled, and in the aftermath of their crash landings, needles and leaves drifted slowly and soundlessly downwards towards a place of rest, while vulture lurked quietly in the shadow of shade.

The rain began, but softly fell, and there was no wind at all. A cool vapor pulled through the campsite, but it was faint and hard to discern. Greet could sense it on her extremities; she wanted the air to cool down, it was too warm to sleep and she was worried about the bugs, but there was no relief that night. She lay in wait. A white hat was placed carefully on a tree branch near the entrance to her campsite and her dress, a delight of shiny, satiny, embroidered pearly frock lay strewn on the ground. Near the vines was her bug box and inside, her current companion, a scorpion.

Her guests arrived and found her lying in an over-stuffed upholstery chair deep inside a room of mangrove raised high upon stilts. She looked so seductive and the hunters dropped their shotguns, and then they came to her, one by one, the hunters without their guns. Her fancy dress shoes dangled and hooked from her feet, extending through a tangle of vine. Her long legs were veiled in fishnet stockings and her well-manicured, yellow-painted toenails pushed past the tiny peeps of her pretty shoes. Through the sheerness of her stockings brightly-polished, creamy painted sunflower points reached and scratched a hunter's leg and, one by one, she turned on them and killed the murderers, one by one.

An early morning woke, beckoning the sun, and when day broke large numbers of vulture swooped down from night perches and undressed the plume hunters, neatly folding their clothes − later to be shipped back to their families, along with pieces of identifying bone.

Others flew off and gathered their relatives together for a big feast. Wings of thousands circled and descended, for a sky burial had commenced. They performed ritual purification and hopping and jousting and tugging and pulling they swarmed for a piece of meat and, passing the plate, splattered blood and guts everywhere. They tore, ripped, and snapped sinew and entrails like rubber balloons, swallowing bits of mangled corpse, leaving skeletal carcasses and bodies without heads and everyone ate and shared the carrion that had been heaped in a pile during the night.

But the plume hunters had not expected to be killed. In reality, Greet's motive, revenge, was dwarfed by her motive to bring long lost relatives back to life for they had messages to share and could show survivors the way for what they had seen and experienced was extraordinary indeed.

For years, science tried hard to figure how to bring people back from the dead and awaken their old lives . . . as they were . . . and many were just lying around, waiting for that scientific breakthrough. Extinct animals and slaughtered birds laid in wait too, in the ground, by way of peoples' violent nature, and greed. But with prayer and chant, the dead came back to life. Science didn't really understand, understand at all, that all a person needed to do was journey . . . they were already here.

The night woke to a dripping draught. Moist, saturated air filled the space beyond Greet's tent. She rose and stepped out into a fragrant vapor of exotic hardwood and watched as sunshine sketched out a tropical floor. Conscious of her movements, she moved as if a man who appreciated beauty was always watching her. She was accustomed to intoxicating men and entrancing them; watched by men who appreciated beauty and, hunted and stalked all her life, they seemed, always, downwind from her scent . . . She bent over a bowl filled with cool water and stooping towards daybreak's ablution, cupped her hands and, raising them in baptism, rinsed the evening from her face.

A one-eyed toad hopped into her tent, it had visited before. Each time it came she placed it gently outside, on another path: she didn't want to roll over and squish it.

Greet was running now and cars and trucks shared the road with her. Drivers slowed down to take a look then speeding up drove off.

Chapter 10

Occo knew Lithil picked through trash cans and thought it good there were trash cans to pick through.

In 2025, the President of the United States granted to globalists all the land that had been occupied by the American people for close to 400 years, by way of an open border policy. A dominant, international trade agreement and monopoly was created, usurping American sovereignty and the top predators, the greedy fat ducks, were out hunting what was left of the big game now.

Why did the government give away the land to the entire world? Why not return it to the first people and make things whole . . . you know . . . try and heal? Ptarro thought. *Who in tarnation did they think they were?*

Americans had managed to survive, though their numbers greatly diminished. Occo began, "The Wilderness League began to teach, Lithil. It instructed the greatest storytellers among them to empower all creatures and, importantly, to use North American story motifs so people could relate and better understand how endangered they all were, and make changes for the better, because if they were not careful they would lose it all to greed and waste and global thieves."

"Well, come on, open the book," demanded Lithil.

Ptarro arrived and Wishtonwish scrambled out from behind the big-rock meeting place. He had been waiting a long time.

Ptarro was carrying a transistor radio and listening to a talk show. It was the anniversary of the sale of Maplewood to the Chinese and there was still a lot of discussion over the loss of critical food supplies in the nation. The radio broadcast had alerted Wishtonwish to his approach: wherever there was political tension, one could always find Ptarro.

"What happened, Ptarro? What happened in DC?"

"Oh, Geela was canned. Her life's in danger."

"Well, she's got plenty of courage, Ptarro. Treasury has wanted to get rid of her for so very long now. But why toss her out? What's the point? Most of them lobbyists and their clients, heck, they still get everything they want, don't they? What's left to be had, that is?"

"Oh, I don't know. Like Geela said ever since them guys broadcast money seed insiders were so busy caressing and kissing one another and dividing the power and wealth, they just weren't paying attention and Geela . . . well, it's possible she was just a foregone conclusion."

"But it's different now. They're distracted, not at ease. I mean, take a look at DC – it's in shambles. I guess it's not nearly as much fun for them, or profitable, as it was creating a class of serfs. A little like playing chess without the pawns."

"You never told me what happened in Maplewood. I want to know. Was Bow Darrel's niece with you in Virginia?"

Ptarro sighed and sat down at the big-rock meeting place. He dropped his pack to the ground and turned off his radio. He said nothing while Wishtonwish built a fire and cooked the evening meal.

After a while Ptarro unpacked and while eating cocked his head and considered Wishtonwish, his little friend.

They sat around the campfire and Ptarro began.

"We were hiding in them shadbushes, over there, along the banks of that river," Ptarro tossed his head, indicating the general direction, "in the east. What's its name? The James . . . I think."

"We were spying on the Chinese buyers and Maplewood shareholders. They were havin' a private meeting not many knew about . . . most learnt about it later, readin' the papers."

Ptarro stretched his legs and wings and cast his eyes towards the night sky. Silence passed between them. "Maplewood is upriver from the Chesapeake, Wish, and it is home to the planet's largest repository of pork products."

"A long time ago, men there started a meat packing company. Two enterprising men," he paused a minute, contemplating. "Heck, if you think about it, this whole country was built on the backs of working people . . . don't you ever forget that, Wish."

"Well, anyway, those enterprising folk in Maplewood had always contributed to the country's larder and it *was* home to America's largest meat packing company, until the Chinese bought it."

Lithil sat up straight in her chair and asked, "How'd this happen?"

"Easy, the Chinese used the mock it got from selling Americans made-in-china junk and bought a very large part of America's food supply in Maplewood."

"How?"

"Oh my Agod, are they ever clever Lithil. They beat us at our own game . . . and with the mock they picked right off of those trees."

"But mock has no value now," Occo continued. "Plants have value, water and seeds have value, and other things like minerals and salts. A world of extreme numbers and big appetites, a world built amongst dwindling resources, whose transactions were supported by mock was bound to fail. It couldn't endure and its end was an ugly one; *oh, my brother, in concordance, my brother slain me."*

"Pork is that other white meat delicacy, don't you know?" Ptarro laughed. "Heck, Maplewood is the largest pork producer in the whole wide world."

Wishtonwish tilted his head and wondered at Ptarro. "I heard the talks were in the way back of a barn yard . . . millions of chickens wandering around every whichy way, screeching and squawking, feathers flying everywhere."

"Yes, it was just like that, only more so, surreal . . . frantic . . . hasty even. I can still see it . . . and Wreda, well, she'd never seen anything like it. Chicken delegates had gathered from all across America to represent China's interest."

"I had heard that . . . so many chickens and all of them hoping if the bid was successful then finally, maybe, they'd no longer be the number one go-to food on the planet . . . what were they thinking?" Wishton mused aloud.

Ptarro puffed out his chest, fluffing his pride with feathers and plenty of authority. "They were thinking more white pig meat would be eaten than white chicken meat, of course and they were glad to be emissaries, happy to oblige, feeling hopeful for a minute. But their government used guile and seduction and they were tricked and double-crossed. The human population was growing and exploding so fast that owning the biggest pig producer couldn't do them chickens no good, no more."

Wishtonwish pondered before he spoke again.

"A foreign investment committee quietly approved the sale. There was no opposition from any group in North America, you know, tryin' to block the deal . . . none that we knew about anyway. That's what the media reported."

"'Don't believe a word you read in the papers or hear on TV,' ain't that what Geela always says?"

Ptarro reflected before continuing. "What a disappointment, really; Geela told Wreda and me to spy on them chickens and get the skinny, and we did. She understands the big picture. Heck . . . I certainly don't."

Ptarro thought some more then said, "You know Wish, them Chinese wanted a future where they could eat meat every day just like we did. But Geela believes America should own its own food supplies . . . as do many others. She was sure globalism would fail . . . and in a big way."

"Furthermore," Ptarro went on, "allowing interests from other countries to buy our assets . . . into our food supply . . . well, it was a lousy, bad idea."

Wishtonwish timidly asked, "So, Ptarro, how did you fall?"

Ptarro sighed. "Wreda and me, we had a plan. She changed shape and got inside the barnyard—no one knew the difference—and passed me intelligence. I encoded it and sent it to members of the Wilderness League."

"I was all set and ready, clinging to a high wire strung on a utility pole connected to hundreds of other poles spread all across the country. My job was to scratch out messages concerning the negotiations at Maplewood."

"High-wire drawing is my adaptive nature, you see, ever since I fell. Why, birds have been congregating on wires ever since wires were strung on all those poles placed along all them railroad lines and roads. Heck, we know more about human activity than the NSA."

Wishtonwish smiled. He knew a lot about human activity too, living in fracking sewers for as long as he had . . . and with his new found activism he had learned even more.

"Most of my signals were sent to this one guy . . . I forget his name. I met him once. Oh, what was his name? He was riding a horse and singing . . . right, I remember, Ligatus Latin, that's it. Red-headed guy somehow involved in the League . . . skinny, with a red beard, long, thin, clean-looking guy. I can see him now, his red beard blowing in the wind, dark eyes, the hair on his head shorn short, and small, black disc earrings, circular and thin, in his earlobes. The wind was flapping through his trouser legs and lifted his light coat right off his frame. He cut a remarkable figure . . . sitting on that horse; my, oh, my, yes sir, he did."

"Anyway, he decoded the signals I scratched out and hand-wrote notes for birds to carry to and fro and devised optical code for fireflies and bats and bees to use in relay. Clever man, he is Wish. But it was Bow Darrel who carried messages to Geela. Bow's her top man."

"Anyway, I clung to this one high wire stretched between poles that followed a river that followed a road that was probably built when horses moved goods round the country, for all I know. Well, I'm a raptor, you know, and can't fly no more, but I am not useless. You see, this one left wing of mine was broke, early on, during that damn Maplewood campaign, so I had to improvise. I managed a pole climb and at the top curled my claws round the rod's circumference, like this a-here, and slid, with my wings tucked, like a skater glidin' along on ice. As a wire-puller, you see, I undulated and swung and moved like the most graceful skater you ever seen. My job was to scratch the encoded messages to others in the group, Geela's group of intelligence gatherers, all members of the Wilderness League."

Eyes twinkling he said, "I looked good up there Wish."

Ptarro continued. "Heck, we all work for Geela, don't we? She's an eagle and has been at this since the beginning . . . involved in building the country, and all of that. She is Agod's daughter and I suspect she's seen a lot, a lot more than me. Me, I mind my own business, I don't represent America or nothing like that. But she does. Heck, her face represents the country to the whole world. Think of that."

"Like I said wire-drawing is my adaptive nature . . . you know . . . ever since I fell. I got to climb poles using my beak and claws, you see, like this a-here, but heck . . . it's okay."

"Wreda told you to buck up, be a man about it," Wish interrupted. "She told me a drone knocked you out of that tree."

"Oh, well, I seen it too but didn't want to say," his voice trailed off. "I was scared, but that little girl, she ain't scared of nothing Wish. To be honest I was feeling a little sorry for myself. But me and her, we didn't discuss it. The drone, that is."

With his tongue in his cheek he said, "My cover was a bird in the bush, but that drone found me, somehow it seen me. I don't rightly know how but, yup, I was shot down by a one of Tossherrheim's corporate drones. There's no doubt about it."

Ptarro was nearly done talking.

"Most of us in the group believe America should own its own food supplies, and Maplewood was selling to the Chinese. Maybe that's why I was shot down . . . heck, I don't know . . . but that's corporatists for you," he shrugged.

"Chickens held big powwows all that year. Thousands of chickens from all over the country were assembling and protesting, moving around and meeting in secret and oh my Agod, it was so out of character for chickens to be political. And all the talking . . . heck, the airwaves were jammed. That's how we got tipped off."

"Don't forget Wish, the Chinese control a major US meat supplier now and they like to keep their food alive till just before cooking. There is a message hidden in all this."

Wreda Blord secretly recorded most of the negotiations. She took good notes. Her annotations named the big banks and cartel interests who were selling off American assets. She identified the chief players and the enabling government regulators. A multinational global cartel had used mock to buy everything out from under ordinary people, making serfs of them.

The Wilderness League was learning so much. Banks no longer controlled the flow of capital and government was just a printing press for big corporations who controlled everything—seeds, water . . . all of it—and securitized the whole planet.

Tossherrheim, a chief antagonist and a leader of international globalists, was hiding behind the big-rock meeting place and had heard everything Ptarro said. He manipulated states on behalf of globalists' interests—trade, migration, and politics—and had tracked Ptarro since the sale of Maplewood.

I want that magic book, dammit. In it are past, present, and future. I don't want it to fall into the wrong hands . . . and I'm gonna kill you and your little buddy Wishyton if I don't get it soon.

Only recently had Tossherrheim learned that there was an entire league devoted to reclaiming the continent in order to save the land and its people from extinction, and from corporatists too, and he kicked up his game.

Back in DC the sun began to set. Lithil and Occo put the book down and, because it only worked in sunlight, they sat in the window and waited for morrow.

Chapter 11

"Geela didn't find what she was looking for at Jekyll," Occo said. "The inn there was shuttered and closed. Treasury's ancestral aristocrats had drifted into the dunes of a shifting landscape and vanished."

"But Papel and Stoonman were there. They hid, in the same way lobbyists hid and concealed the identities of their clients, and with deceit helped them steal the country's wealth with mock. They pretended to be Geela's friends, old aristocrats, but Papel and Stoonman were corporate agents. They grabbed Geela, took her to old New York, dumped her down a dungeon, and left her to vanquish and die."

Stoonman still owned a car and took it out for a spin whenever gasoline was available. It was a 1950's American classic, a red, wing-tipped beauty of an automobile with a special plate, SNITCH. It identified him as a corporate agent and allowed him to pass on the roads. The car had a white rag top with white-walled tires and a little sticker decal with the word SNIFF stuck on its rear window. Raunchy sex music, with explicit lyrics, blasted from the radio; a fortunate youth, cruising fast . . . *boom boom boom* . . . enjoying the cold sunshine . . . *boom boom boom* . . . lapping up what the world had to offer a potent, young, American male. His cheek filled with an omnipresent pop and he used his tongue and teeth to swish and swirl it about, exclaiming his sex and virility.

Stoonman looked at a woman's ass first, then her face. In his mind women who wore trousers were, rightfully so, as concerned about their presentation to the world as he was and glanced behind at their reflections at home, before leaving the house. But between Stoonman and his accomplice, Papel, there was a chasm. Papel was a man who appreciated the way a dress hung on a woman's frame, her face, her beauty. He did not idolize a woman's butt end.

Papel grabbed Geela, threw her in the back of his car and snapped a tracking device around her ankle. Geela was upset. With great circular sweeps her wings signaled her anxiety and, impatient and disappointed in herself, she slapped and banged as she paced and thrashed against the windshield, in the rear.

Lately there were more hours in the day, but this year the warmth was taking longer to arrive than the light, and the weather outside suddenly turned cold. After some time they stopped at a roadside tavern; a painting of an old wooden dock, zig-zagging over a submerged marshland that extended out past a squishy earth of salt hay, hung in its window. Inside, wine guzzlers, beer drinkers, singers and dancers, drug addicts—all kind of rowdy folk—crowded into a tight bar space, intoxicated past pleasure. Vomit and smoke filled the room. The place was an exchange, the economic heart of the nearby region, a lively market for trade in people . . . sex anyway you liked it . . . drugs, medicine, and all kinds of security. Its streets were patrolled at night by corporate police and it was a very dangerous place.

A woman was leaning with her back against a wall, one leg bent at the knee, the other foot flat on the floor, smoking tobacco, casually surveying the action at the tables and around the larger room. *Oh my Agod, what these people don't do on the table they do under it,* the woman said to herself.

Someone else was rolling a cigarette. She lit it and pulled a strand of tobacco hair from her front tooth. A young woman was stooped over, dressing her baby, while a man behind her scratched his chest and stooped down to eat food that had fallen on the floor. Another man with a cloth over his head inhaled from a pipe and several women took off their clothes and danced on a table top. An old man was stomping his feet and threw his arms up in the air, exclaiming mirth and good cheer. A few looked at Papel and Stoonman but only because they were traveling with an eagle – heck, for the most part, most were too drunk to distinguish one from the other.

Geela recognized the woman leaning against the wall and watched as she took finely-cut tobacco leaf from a bag and rolled cigarettes into elegant sticks, but did not acknowledge her. Cril Wrog was her name and her attraction was not unlike that of a wild creature. She set out to meet men the way a heated animal attracts a mate, making a trail of her scent.

Inside the hall, rolling tobacco in thin cigarette paper, smoking obliquely, casually sipping from a bottle of beer, Cril watched and waited. Soon enough Stoonman caught her scent and, sniffing, sauntered over to where she stood. She shook her hair free from her face the way young women do when the eyes of men are upon them and they, without a word, consent to the looking. He leaned and spoke into her ear over the loud music blasting from the juke box and asked her for a light . . . Stoonman was a tobacco smoker too.

Cril Wrog pressed her body into the curve of the bar while his eyes hastily scanned the features of her face, and she worked fast. There, in that bar amongst a shocking bunch of people, Crila, as her friends like to call her, seduced Stoonman in the men's bathroom and while they were fiercely fornicating, patrons slipped in and out of the door and didn't seem to notice. She deposited her scent on him and Crila could now find him wherever he wandered: she had left an indelible mark, nature's tracking device. He was smitten and a one-way fixation began that would lead him astray, and in a big way.

Papel, much older, lurked elsewhere; he was curious and, as many had abandoned tracking technology, he gathered information the old-fashioned way, by asking questions. Oh, he had seen Crila too. He felt her eyes upon his back and her ears listening to the inflections in his voice while he and Stoonman casually chatted. Arm crooked, dangling a cigarette, he hovered at the fringe of conversations, seemingly aloof yet most certainly engaged. Humored and bored with the attention women extended him all his life, he was suddenly confounded and unable to brush her presence aside.

Something about her—she was young, bold-spirited, and beautiful—was choking him. She couldn't possibly know any better what she thought she could change, could she? No. Too young to know better he decided, too inexperienced. She was just beginning to get an impression of things.

Geela sat at a window. She peered out through its icy panes. Across from her the men were still eating. A spring squall was kicking up outside and a cold, strong wind whirled, scratching a frosty film on the window panes. A fire burned in the hearth, casting warmth and yellow light about the room. A street lamp's dim beam streaked and, slanting towards the interior through a pattern of reticulated plate, scattered dust and low voice about her while outside the blowy, howling wind blew a fierce fugue.

Geela tilted her head and considered the glass in her hand, nearly empty, and in the warm, pleasant respite of a place in her mind its sentient effect insulated her from the outside world, but storm tugged. The northerly wind stimulated and stirred her body, altering the moment. Gazing through watery bourbon past a lipstick-smeared rim, the outside world, and, oh yes, her life, beckoned. But what could she do now, she wondered, looking over at her captors?

Papel rose and stepping over vomit and fornicators spoke aloud to the spectators in the bar, "Look who I have here, the great American eagle whose head is on nearly every dollar ever printed," and some in the crowd heard him and were interested enough to approach for a closer look.

Geela's head dropped. Tossherrheim suddenly appeared and placed himself between the boys and, addressing them by their first names, shouting over all the noise, even laughing a little, slapped Stoonman and his friend firmly on their backs and said, "Come on now, I've been looking for you. I've got some work that needs to be done," and as Geela didn't have the magic book, Tossherrheim told the two where to dump her, shook their hands and said goodbye.

Before he left the tavern, Tossherrheim revealed his plot to stop Geela, to stop Wishtonwish, to stop Ptarro and thwart any effort by the Wilderness League to save the land and its people from extinction and take the country back from globalists and restore Agod to power, not mock. Privately, Tossherrheim was worried there would be trouble with Agod over this.

Old New York City was a morgue now, and mostly under water. New New York City had moved to the northwestern hills of Jersey, not far from where the new New York City mega-rich kept their current refugee camp, near Trenton.

When they arrived in old New York, they watched as piles of dead fat people were stuffed into suitcases, their corpulent, greasy flesh oozing from bulging seams, stacked high on docks outside a dungeon door. They watched in amazement as undertakers slid thousands of makeshift coffins down a plank and plopped them into the sea . . . straight from dock to sea.

Some of the fat ones were fed to the unfortunate ones condemned to live in the dungeons of old New York; they had either eaten way too much and died, all-of-a-sudden like, from the shock and news that food was scarce or were captured and put inside the gaol to be eaten alive by wharf rats or gnawed on by the condemned.

When Geela saw this she vowed she'd eat only wharf rats. Ampersand had been here. She had heard his story and knew what to expect. He had prayed to Agod, promising to eat less and live Another Way, and somehow he escaped and lived to tell.

The rodents were well-fed, indeed. Geela skinned the living rats alive. She disemboweled them first then ate their brains, a delicacy, and then she ate their flesh. It was the only food Geela had and those stuck in the dungeons had to eat something: either fat people, alive or dead, or rats who ate fat people, dead or alive. The choice was easy for Geela.

Chapter 12

Ptarro heard all the stories, all of them, but never run across any red ants. When they weren't dousing flames in the canyons or fighting fires in the forest or tending the funeral pyres of great animals, the specially equipped little pissants were urinating in the dry, scorched agricultural districts around the country, fertilizing the fields; otherwise they preferred to be left alone.

Ptarro tried to put Maplewood behind him and in the morning he and Wish set out early for the ant colony. A few days passed and it was easy going, but Ptarro's spirits remained low, and his mind continued to suffer.

"This walking crap is for the birds," he said to Wishtonwish after a while, "and, anyway, who come up with an expression like that? Some guy on two legs? And what does it mean, Wish?"

Wishtonwish didn't answer, but scurried along beside him. He had had enough of the dark side of Ptarro. West of Middle River the terrain was rougher and the walking tougher and despite careful maneuvering it tore at Ptarro's heels, his claws were scratched and bloodied, his toe nails ripped and torn. He was tormented. His mood did not improve and, just when he thought he couldn't take another step, he heard singing. Its voice seemed to come from out of the clouds, and it surrounded him. Ligatus Latin just happened to be riding nearby on his horse and offered to give him a lift.

Ligatus was a red-haired, skinny guy who encoded secret messages for the League and when he wasn't working counterintelligence he rode his horse all over the land. A ring of bats was always circling about him and used their purple tongues to lick salt from off his skin, and from off his horse too.

Ligatus was a welcome sight for Ptarro's sore feet. Hope bloomed o'er his face and as they rode closer and closer to the ant colony he looked up, and ahead, before them, the frontier appeared, its border a precipice thrusting into the clouds. He shouted, "Oh, my aching feet, will you look at that!"

Ligatus Latin said, "This is where you get off, buddy, my horse won't climb no higher."

Down he hopped and Ligatus rode off singing and his horse sang along too . . . in two-part harmony.

A water-eroded ravine with a dry riverbed separated them from the eastern wall ahead. They slipped and slid a butt slide down, plowing the earth with their heels, loose soil and rock running ahead. Stones rolled and announced their approach, the sounds hollow and dry as Ptarro and Wishtonwish crossed the arroyo and began their ascent.

They scaled the high, eastern flank and grabbing saplings for balance, crawled past boulders, losing footholds in slides and slippery setbacks. Wishtonwish scrambled along but sweat trickled off Ptarro's beak. He was straining and struggling, his breathing a pant. He crawled towards the crest and after the long walk from Virginia was exhausted but with a final hoist managed to pull himself up onto the summit and, trembling, stood on wobbly legs.

Oh my Agod, oh my . . . below, out of nowhere, rose the prospect of a river and what an enchanting scene it was − from the ridge top, such splendor. Gurgling currents giggled, and carelessly curled around scattered sandstone. Sun beams bent at the river's surface, their winking stars shining, shimmering and dazzling, beholding his eyes. Minstrels and troubadours wore yellow and silver, swimming this way and that, fins upon the cool river water. A lovely melody sang and its music lured him − tinkling, tubular, glass whirls of wind and its sweet, strophic song healed Ptarro, shaking off the difficult journey and defeat he suffered in Maplewood. Lone swan, uncoupled and oblivious, swam on past, heading towards an opposite bank. Nature exalted, and Ptarro stayed.

Chapter 13

Hoarfrost on the fields, mottled white soared. A few late apples clung silently to trees sentried against the expanse and water-color streaked gray and turquoise across a big sky.

Winter approached. Wreda ran through the Appalachian snow, past red osier and patient rhododendron. Past, present and future displayed along the route and no imagination at all was required to notice that present imposed upon the past and hinted at what was to come.

The cold, crisp soundlessness broke. Geese flew overhead, honking noisily, invading the airspace. The flock was friendly, part of the Wilderness League's group of allies. In colder months the honkers fed in the lower states and for the privilege provided good intelligence on the Canadian interior. They told Wreda she was needed by the Mackinac Boat People, and quick.

Wreda Blord jogged along a rural route once occupied by motor vehicles, past frost-covered fields and an occasional farm. On the side of the road a young woman was working on a car, bent over its engine, under a hood. An American flag flapped outside her worn, rundown house and out in front grew a plant whose intelligence she let influence her. She steeped the plant's leaves and drank the tea to sleep, it promoted visions in dreamtime and she could see like an owl. Wreda recognized it. She used wormwood too.

A breathless morning, amorphous clouds floated on a horizon barely discernible and gathering and swirling at shape-shifting altitude, gray had motion, moved swiftly now, washed then clean.

On the ground there was no wind and running was warm work for Wreda, her upper legs powerful with too many field mice and meadow rats. She was barred owl and on her way to Vancouver to visit her uncle, Bow Darrel, and planned to run the entire distance there. She dragged her drooping wings and, exhaling heavily, exerted enormous effort, struggling to run. Flying had made her fat, easily plucking rodents from bountiful fields, and she must work extra hard to keep her body fit. On her way to Vancouver by way of the Great Lakes, she had embarked upon a physical fitness regime and rushed past fields in the countryside that, beyond green, beyond the brilliant joyful color bursts of autumn, fell into brown and naked, waited for snow.

Wreda slept beneath an autumnal canvas of foliage, and in the morning threw off the leaves she had used for cover and heaved her body from off the ground. She could still do this at her advanced age—true, it was a big effort—her mother could only dream about it, but Wreda was happy.

Wreda ran past an old foundation . . . a root cellar or shelter lined with stones. Inside grew the absinthe plant. She saw signs of harvest and gathered some herself. A white birch had toppled in a shearing wind and its halved height stood alongside a broken section in the wall. It seemed marten had been climbing and at the place where it tore, a brown smear splattered and a mark remained. Its spirit spilled a talisman and left the dark stain and smiling to herself, she thought it a good sign.

Wreda was Lithil, and the young woman whose car didn't run. After some time Wreda ran back to the car and got it going while the young woman sat inside, and dreamed.

She flew and traveled fast, faster than she could see. Oh, light rays bent and sparked their beams, but the path they lit was dim. Power lines obstructed and she struggled to wrest free . . . she must get clear and free. The landscape careened and path to vision stalled, but then light kindled an electric impulse and image paused, put on a mask, and waited for her to see.

It was risky but eyes rewound and, developing over time, adjusted to the light and all time she could see. She made it through, free and clear, of wire traps and snares, and flew. Loose of it she veered, past tanglement, and soared; yes, high now, she was free.

Below a woman with white hair was driving a white pickup truck—she looked to be eighty, maybe ninety years old—and was wearing a baseball cap and driving on the wrong side of the road, paying no mind at all to those shouting expletives at her. Wreda wondered if she, in the end, would be like her, and live long enough to drive on the wrong side of the road.

The clouds moved at furious speed. She couldn't see as clearly as she'd like . . . but good enough. Rose bushes rode with the old woman . . . in the back, on the truck bed, small fragile buds, compact plants, strong in the wind, on the ride of their lives, a bedful of rose, transplanted beauty on the wrong side of the road. It was a glad sight – shrubs in bloom, past bud, fragrance wafting, shuddering, shaking, shivering, live beauty, like livestock in the back of a moving truck, bending and blowing in the wind on the wrong side of the road . . . then light soaked the shining rose and somehow moved the sun.

Wreda stopped to rest. She found a still pool in a swift river and bathed in it alone, and the water in the stream poured westward way on into another clear stream and then another.

It was late afternoon and she oriented herself towards the sun, its heat severely angled on a beam glaring from out of the west. It met her eye hard and, blocking its blinding ray with a wing, she looked out over all the hundreds of rounded stones in the stream bed, so perfectly shaped—there were tens of thousands of them—and watched the water on its journey and, as it traveled along, wash and playfully plop, shooting joyfully into the air off the rounded stones. In the water play insects as white as light floated and filled the air space above, circling and hovering in accompaniment.

Next day she found herself at the Great Lakes. The Mackinac Boat People who lived there embodied coyote philosophy and were habituated, accustomed to human presence. Coyotes were active day and night, year round, and so were the Mackinacs. They bred in February and March, so did the Boat People. Coyotes arranged their family groups around an alpha male and female and so did those living on boats, and all the lakes were their territory.

Chicago bankers were still exchanging mock for things, but the Mackinac Boat People were peculiarly adaptable, active day and night, and year round, and had little use for money. A light-skinned, dark man with green eyes like a lizard spoke for the people, he was their alpha male.

He complained about coyote. Coyote was eating their food. Wreda suggested they stop feeding coyote and coyote would go on its way. Green Eyes said Boat People don't feed coyote. "Oh, yes, you do," she said, "scavengers live in a much smaller world than you imagine."

"Move your bird feeders. Birds scatter seed on the ground and stray seeds attract rodents and small rodents attract coyote and fisher and hawk and owl, for that matter," Wreda continued. "Look, there are hundreds of wild animals in the cities – they go where the food is. When I am in the wilderness, outside city perimeters, along the trails and in the hills, I just don't see them in large numbers like I see them in the cities. So get rid of your bird feeders and move your trash to a place where you want coyote to be."

Some transient Macs traveled hundreds of miles looking for new territory; they did not all live on the water in boats. These ones replaced themselves in less than a year. It was tough on the water, but tougher on land. Prey abounded, yes, it was plentiful in rural and suburban areas but breeding pairs needed many miles of forest to feed their families and sometimes snatched domestic pets and babies, causing hysteria among their neighbors. They hunted with reloaded cartridges and foraged for mushrooms and berries and, trapping fish in weirs, survived anyway they could and, like a lot of other people in the parklands, were content.

The people on the Great Lakes assisted those crossing the straight, Macs controlled it and charged a toll to cross, but as they had no use for mock asked Wreda for advice. She suggested they trade and engage in barter and exchange, for the things they needed in order to live well and survive, and so they did.

Many making the cross were on their way to Sequoia where the Happy People lived. Happy People were a tribe of fearless, awesome warriors who lived in trees. Life expectancy was longer there and Mackinac met a lot of people on their way, in search of a longer more meaningful life. Travelers stopped and stayed awhile and shared story around their campfires at night and, occasionally, a coyote left and went to live in the trees.

Chapter 14

Bow Darrel had a letter for Ptarro. It was from Geela and as he had no intelligence on Ptarro or his whereabouts, Bow was not sure whither he wandered, the letter remained undelivered for some time. But Bow was tired of looking for the old bird, it was wearing him down.

Darrel was Geela's top man and flew surveillance over the land, with Fig Sherkin, a kingfisher from Columbia River. Fig was a big help, but Bow, he was top man.

Bow Darrel and Fig Sherkin surveyed abandoned fracking sites where hundreds of abandoned well heads lay idle, littered with wrecked remnants of equipment, but just today, for some reason, at one of these facilities, machines were up and running. Fig heard creaking noises, the bumping and squeaking clank of worn metal against rusty metal. He smelled the sweet, nauseating odor of diesel fuel and it was making him sick.

Fig vomited in mid-air as he rattled over to Bow, "What's that noise, and what's that awful smell?"

Darrel slowed to a hover. This place had been abandoned for a long time, but now steam shovels and big pieces of heavy equipment were pooping toxic stuff through vertical orifices and low extensions of exhaust pipes. His bulging, bulbous eyes—he used his own binocular lenses for economy—ogled the deteriorating wellhead and quickly snapped several aerial photos. He saw Ampersand, scout for the Cold People, riding about on a bicycle, and a group of survivors who were huddled together around a neglected drill shaft seeking heat. Ampersand rode all over the country, trading junk he found in rubbish heaps for fruit, vegetables, and nuts, and meat and fish, whatever he could get. He was a scout for the Cold People and Cold People were scavengers.

Bow was seeing more and more of this kind of thing at abandoned fracking sites. Folks long accustomed to central heat didn't want to live without it and wherever they could, built makeshift colonies and small outdoor furnace operations and clustered around open pits. Cold People tended to be bitter about their loss, and hadn't pursued Another Way.

On the far perimeter of his radar, Bow saw a faint blip and with a fast, overextended flex quickly adjusted his farsighted focus, sharpening his retinal image and, sure enough, it was Ptarro.

Humph . . . well, whatta you know . . . What's that ol' bird doing so far west and with the ants already? Man, I coulda missed him. If I had rotated one degree less or swiveled any tighter, I'd have missed him. Damn . . . got to be more careful.

Bow was all lathered up, distracted; flustration flushed him and he lost his composure and when he came back around was so pleased he'd found Ptarro that he didn't see what was ahead of him.

"Look out!" shouted Fig, as Bow crashed into a tree.

"Get back to headquarters and send a message to Geela. I found Ptarro," said Bow angrily.

Fig asked, "What do you mean, you found Ptarro? I found Ptarro, you ol' bag of bones."

"I said get back to headquarters and send a message to Geela," and with that tone, Fig nodded and quickly flew away.

Darrel quickly noted the locus of the unclaimed fossil fuels and the incursion of settlers, then seized his chance and, before he could blink his own owl's eye, deftly jagged and swiftly changed course. He hovered briefly and satisfied it was the old bird slumbering beneath him descended silently, swooping down upon the ant colony, and powerfully gliding on majestic, outstretched wings, circled tighter as he approached his target.

In the altitude drop the pouch round his neck swung and bumped chaotically on his breast; his niece, Wreda Blord, had made it with fine feathers and porcupine-quills, and finished off her efforts by stamping his initials 𝘉𝘋 on the top overlap.

He jerked and breathlessly leveled course. Ptarro was swinging low in a hammock, claws curled in the air, snoring away in the afternoon heat. Without a word Bow opened the flap, took the letter from the purse and dropped it on the old bird's chest and snapping a sudden, sharp wing clap, turned to perch on a nearby tree.

The shrill sound of Bow shrieking so near his eardrums rudely awakened him and Ptarro nearly fell to the ground, but while his wits slowly woke, his brainpower roused, sparking and firing as he come round.

"Well, hello Bow, good day to you."

Bow gave Ptarro his orders and was just about to leave but remembered something and said, "Stop in on your way west Ptarro and attend the summit at Great Hall. Agod just returned from the way north and will soon address an assembly in White Tents, around the time of the new moon. And, oh, Geela's returned," and with these words he bid the raptor adieu.

"Geela has returned? Are you kidding me?"

Ptarro struggled with composure as a slow realization swiftly swarmed his sleepy senses. *Why not go?* Ptarro's heart quickened: he wanted to skip a tarantella and dance himself silly.

41

Ptarro stumbled upon the idea that Wreda Blord would be there too. He hopped hastily off his hammock and, as he was particularly keen to see her again, nervously fumbled, nodding a quick reply. He shouted after Darrel, "Yes . . . yes, I'll come."

"My flappin' feathers, why, ha-ha, lots of creatures from round the continent will be there, some I ain't seen in years. Holy Toledo! Sure, I'll be there Bow. Thanks."

Bow smiled knowingly, whistling as he flew away and Ptarro's voice trailed as Bow rose higher and higher into the sky.

Chapter 15

Over a hill a battalion of ants slowly emerged, one by one, off an orange clay road, streaming like ribbons lying along its crest. At the hilltop, against lapis blue banded with white, red armored bodies glinted in sunlight as their long black legs extended and elbowed sideways, nimbly and cautiously crawling forward. On their feet were black boots, loosely laced and untied, their leather tongues drooping in the sweaty dust. Their antennae tugged and yanked toward heaven, snatching tastes and smells from the air and as the army marched westward way low dust clouds followed its trail. The panting ants pulled as the hairy fellers felt ahead, dragging irrigation hose over an arid land. Rubber lines stretched from rivers and lakes over miles of rugged landscape, to farmlands in the thirsty, drought ravaged fields, tracts that had fed millions, but where now the earth was dry and cracked.

Behind them, a road vaulted and fell abruptly towards a river. Marvelously constructed craters of fine powder stood along its banks and riparian ripples littered their dense and sandy dunes. Thousands of troops remained behind, billeted in cones and cavities that tunneled downward to interior rooms where clumps of sticky, white eggs were piled and food was stored. All day long soldier ants, trained in line, carried things in and out, from one place to another, consuming, exhuming, from inside their holes out into the circumference of their world. They heard the sun. And the sun, while traveling its orbit, circling the firmaments, moved and pulled a drape over everything the ants saw and heard.

An old and fearless bird, Ptarro was the battalion's commander, a raptor who couldn't fly. He strode a fair piece in front of his troops, head down, leaning into the distance ahead. Orders had arrived instructing him and his ants to haul water from Middle River, across western terrain to farmlands in California and basins in the Colorado. Geela of White Tents had sent the message and he was asleep in a hammock when it arrived.

But first, a stop at White Tents – the glaciers had all melted and Ptarro liked to see that sort of thing. Plus, Geela had summoned him.

Along the way, Ptarro remembered the first time he met Wreda Blord. It was several years ago and as he trod along he thought long and hard about that day. He had been with Erhon Geren at Green River. They were rummaging through a pile of scrap metal searching for something or other when she first appeared, and immediately he liked her. Later Ptarro wrote to Geela and told her all about Wreda Blord, then contacted his favorite radio station and gave them the story.

We were scavenging near Green River, bent over a pile of scrap metal, digging furiously for an alloy we needed to repair a radio transmitter. But we couldn't find it — there were only tin and aluminum cans in that dump. Frustration had set in and particularly so as Erhon was sure what we needed was there: he could usually find nearly anything humans threw out and thought he knew where all the good stuff was, but this time was not successful.

'North America is a rich repository of trash,' he always said and, why, when Erhon Geren wasn't escorting troops or teaching survivors how to fish he was culling through rubbish heaps, picking through trash, and writing commentary on everything he came across . . . what it was, what it was used for, why it was thrown away. He was writing a book, that boy was, and chronicling the economic history of a nation by examining its trash heaps.

Wreda wandered in on our prospecting . . . we musta looked crazy, digging through that pile . . . and I was embarrassed. But heck I chuckled and said, 'we underground eco-terrorists are not wastrels.'

She looked real good, the hulk of her frame moved seductively when she ran over to greet us and I was smitten . . . hopelessly and unrequitedly attracted to her. We talked for hours and it became clear to me that Wreda was an important soldier in the Wilderness League . . . there were so many talented ones I had not met. She spoke at length of the agricultural tribes and their effort to keep survivors alive and fed. Bee tribes had joined forces with the agricultural tribes and together, for decades, prepared for America's decline. They had collected seeds, phosphorous, and other necessary minerals and anticipated the exodus to the parklands. They were ready. Wreda explained that both ants and bees were rather voiceless masses, necessary but expendable, nevertheless happy and well-looked-after by the agricultural folks and others who pursued Another Way.

Crops in California must be irrigated or everyone living there will starve Wreda said to us. Can it be done and how she asked? She had heard a story about a farmer in California, a girl farmer, who developed a new snack food. She called it Bug Bites. The girl raised insects and when they were fully developed applied a freeze-dried process to the bugs. She treated them with two flavors: savory salts and spice, and sweet honey. Of course, the ants and bees had heard all about it and said it was not enough to sustain a people and privately it repulsed them, but what could they do? They were a voiceless mass, but otherwise well-treated.

44

Chapter 16

"You've heard of the parkland survivors, Lithil?" asked Occo.

"Of course; at first I thought it all nonsense, but now I'm not so sure."

"Then you've heard of Agod. Agod is supreme leader of the Wilderness League, and the League oversees the parklands. Geela is Agod's daughter and her armature of experience hadn't escaped Agod so Agod sent Vrucos and Coverdia to fetch her and bring her home. It was time for her to come home."

"Vrucos and Coverdia are boreal bosses, Agod's knights, crows from the northern forests of Canada. They protect the Wilderness League from its enemies and interlopers. Geela's in White Tents now and will try and help Agod restore the continent to health."

"Well, I could go on and on but the book is alive, not dead Lithil and in it are past, present and future. Shall we open it?"

Lithil shifted and straightened in her seat, reaching for a handful of Bug Bites. She couldn't wait.

The crows flew to old New York. Vrucos was the older of the two and wore a hood and upper mantle a smoky shade of onyx. His capelet was short, iridescent and mottled, but his coattails long, the color of coal. The younger Coverdia was similarly shaded, but had white primary wing feathers, visible only to a few.

In old New York they saw a curious creature running through its streets and immediately recognized the two-spirited beast. Heris carried a violin strapped over a shoulder and alone in the city he and she ran through its streets and subways, over asphalt and below skyscrapers, along abandoned roads and on past the lonely seaport. When the virtuoso stopped to play the crows listened and noted that while he and she played, Heris paused and listened to the echo bounce off the buildings back to asphalt where he and she stood and, to the crows, it seemed Heris responded more to the returning sound than the play.

Vrucos and Coverdia cawed and cawed, calling out: *Heris . . . Heris follow us.* He and she hesitated but crow insisted, swooping lower and lower and, gently steering, Heris slowly veered and stopped where the cold and lonely asphalt ended. Vrucos asked Heris to play at the top of the road that led to the dungeon where Geela was, and he and she consented.

While Heris played Coverdia tossed a glittering object and Vrucos hopped along on the ground, quietly humming to himself. Seeds and crumbs were scattered outside the entrance to the dungeon and a bucket of water set out for drinking. Vrucos gathered crumbs and dropping them into the bucket, soaked and softened his food before he swallowed. He cough-cawed and following with deeper, coarser banter in a lower key, carried three beats, gargled a watery whistle attached to a musical note, and called the other crow away from her play. Coverdia's shiny black beak and beady black eyes were circumspect. She made rapid drills like a woodpecker would deep inside her throat then hopped towards Vrucos. He chased her away. The crows bantered like this for some time, finally stopping to bouse at a puddle near a dripping faucet.

Heris played, and the music bounced back.

Crow perched for millennia o'er the land and, in exhortation, cried out. They posted on freeways and wires, along roads and rail heads, on roofs and inner-city playgrounds. Down and away they lurked along the coastline and, on out past the ocean, they beseeched.

Cawing and reciting so many plaintive prayers, old Vrucos coaxed a beckoned God and reckoned man. Coverdia nodded in agreement and, with a genuflecting bow, bent to embrace a day that would never come again. Her reverent honor bobbed and in homage she kneeled, as the land yielded days that came again and again. Crows beckoned and bobbed and called *caw caw caw caw* impatiently, until hoarse; but who had noticed?

Geela did and came outside. She squatted and sat, on a stoop, squinty-eyed, faced into the sun, her belongings in a sack beside her. She had hid in that abandoned subway for so long, and had been so all alone in old New York that in her confinement Manhattan had sunk under the weight of the tides, and most of old New York had moved west, to the steep little hills of New Jersey, a long way from the rising water.

Coverdia chewed and chewed and freed Geela of a tracking device. They left old New York City, Geela and the black wings, left the city for the forest, and flew over choked streams of asphalt and steel and concrete barriers, over ugly roads, choked cities and choked streams. They coursed for days above nests of spiky leaves. Squirrels scurried from one branch to the next, tree top squirrels perambulating tree top limbs, never touching the ground.

Geela was happy . . . she was going home. She tried hard to leave her experience in old New York behind her, where it belonged. *Like a deer, I am a deer now . . . no . . . I am an owl with a deer-like world view. Don't look back, Geela. A journey sheds like water. Shake it off and move on, be like that deer,* she told herself, *don't look back, deer wouldn't look back.*

When deer encountered a little trouble, some danger in the wood, was stalked by a hunter or tracked by technology and chased, if lucky, it might escape, get clear away, and continue on with life and live. When deer shook the hunter, shook the predator it didn't dwell on almost dead but the triumph of surviving, and resumed, unassumingly so, to graze, to forage, to search for a mate, to breed, to gestate, to care for its young, its everyday way, and didn't dwell on a sportsman's sketch.

Geela's thinking shifted; exploitation of everything, and America's perfection of it, was short-lived because, well, it was almost gone. The country was overrun and overwrought, decayed, and urban and rural poverty persisted. The ports on Atlantic's rim were below her now and what nasty industrial ports they were: slick transportation hubs that had imported and exported, supporting so many greedy, voracious appetites. She dropped altitude and flew through tunnels built under mighty rivers and it blew Geela's mind, really, what men and women had built, but man, how wrong they had got it in the end, with their mock and unlimited greed.

A whelped coyote with eight or ten teats cried out. She had lost her pups and was searching all over; *where are they?* She trotted over hills and slopes and, although the mountains ahead jutted up towards pliant pieces of cloud puff concealing a great challenge, she didn't stop; came the billowing, heavy clouds: white and blue, purple and gray rolling unto themselves, unto everything, then height covered in wispy curls of smoke so white that light slipped through and illuminated the backside of the ridge.

Hounds were out and gave chase. Coyote followed them down a greasy ridge but before she descended looked back and, though she had never seen clouds look like that, paused and rested in peaceful repose. She knew what she was looking at and embraced the mountain tops and after a while she resumed, caressing the earth with her trotting feet.

Running downhill she slipped on a greasy ridge, startling a herd of white tail that quickly and nervously waved. She laughed and as they danced round and round in the dusky light, she saw only white flags but knew who they were and got a little closer, and closer still, and white tail moved in and got close too. Then she laughed again and repeat startled and coiled flags unfurled and this time ran off and those in front, the ones who had performed the first dance, the circular one, turned to look at coyote and moving out, single file, serpentine-like up the hill in the dusk, waved good-bye and as their circle unwound, eight coyote pups, hiding in a pocket of fog revealed as mist floated and crept up the ridge into the forest after the deer.

The hounds stopped baying at a retention wall farther down the hill. It was an old one built into a squeaky earth from discarded railroad ties. The bottom wood was rotting and inside was shelter for creatures big and small and coyote watched as Cotteeman, 400-year-old Cotteeman, crawled out from the shelter and stood in the mist.

Still lower, a group of vultures lurked where people once dwelled and coyote, who didn't normally get to see this kind of thing, serf country, took a detour round.

The buzzards postured, dozens of them, on rolling, grassy knolls, perching on recumbent limbs that had fallen in the past. A thicket of live oak shielded a littered place but when wind tossed their limbs, flickering light revealed a concealed spot where trees stood, risen from a flood.

About forty buzzards posted while others roosted on the bridge – fishing was not allowed from this point on. They guarded from an abandoned, deteriorated fence, with no rails or wire, only pieces of sagging boards, while, over there, flapping, white-winged fingertips scooped over the land.

The place was a dump, *not my territory*, coyote thought. *This is serf country*, and moved on.

Geela heard running water and stopped to take a drink and as she approached the watering hole, deep inside a narrow gorge, a hawk was there, drinking from her spot. She watched as it flew and left the embedded stream cut through the jagged, rigid place. The creek was running hard, its sound was deafening and its crashing, its rushing water, its thunder and her proximity to the creek were such that Geela couldn't hear the wind blowing or the crows in the trees above. She could see the tree tops swaying and watched their violent moves but couldn't hear over creek roaring loudly with water running off this mountainside. It smelled good. Bats were flying overhead. They liked her and licked her eagle body with their purple tongues.

She wandered, not far from the creek, and took a little walk to a quieter place and found so many there: titmice, robins, chipping sparrows and red-bellied woodpeckers, juncos, flocks of them and the greener cardinal too. They were all here in this quiet place, a little farther from the stream, red cardinals in red sumac, out of the screaming wind.

Tight spot by the creek bed, there were no songbirds there, but here the place afluttered with them as she approached. Lingering leaves rustled a welcome and while birds flocked to greet her and flittered ahead and led, others followed in the flank, first back-tracking to whence she had come. More flew quietly and singularly in tree tops and, watching and accompanying in a circumspect bird-way, kept her safe from harm.

The crows sat bare in naked trees. Vrucos held a yuletide bulb and Coverdia a lantern of light. High above the white earth smoke in amongst the wet, black timber,

December shone in a boggy area along a highway merged. Heading west the crows climbed the Appalachian Mountains; over the hill was warmer still, bright and sunnier too. A covey of pigeon spotted them come cross the range and flew so fast to be of service and race with crow and, flanking them, escorted Geela to the other side; they loved it more and felt the thrill, the whole distance through.

They talked now amongst themselves of the brave people, extraordinary human beings, among the parkland survivors. Brave people had got a lot of people thinking about things so many of them knew, but couldn't articulate. They got people thinking about media and all their lies, make-believe money and the unreal mortgages on their futures and arbitraged standards of living, their children's too, impossible to pay. Corporatists like Tossherrheim with their goals of ruling the world had made serfs out of most and it wasn't a dream . . . no one was making this up.

Geela sighed. The big shots had tried to expropriate the whole world, where it could, not for humanity, but for power and wealth. What had it profited the elites to gain the whole world and lose Agod in the process?

Below, the natural world revealed for them who would not see. They saw through earth and into ground where survivors stored things underground.

They watched as food and clothing were distributed among the survivors. It had been a good year and the Wilderness League practiced cooperation and sharing with those who cultivated an appreciation for the Sun Life, and all that it meant. Gathering and redistributing, trading and bartering among those in the parklands guaranteed rightful heirs their fair share around the continent when the going got tough. They did not feed the milksops, however, the entitled, imperious brats, wholly useless and incapable, but divided tribute between the tribes and traded the fat ones for peace.

Next crow flew over the part of the country where the wind stopped blowing, it never blew . . . all done blowing . . . and the sun didn't shine. It had rained here last night, like spider webs it rained. It sounded like spider webs, it made contact with the spongy, earthy, organic soil like spider webs and its sticky gauze pulled and sounding like spider webs retreated . . . and the rain yanked hard but still adhered to the earth.

Oh, earth still tilted here, one way or the other, the way it always did, to the north or to the south, one way stunting the days shorter and colder the other way growing them longer and warmer till a jarring, jagged tilt hit and shook loose tides that raised the waters with no end in sight.

Along the way, running-out-of-food kind of people, over-consuming types without penitence, gathered in large mobs and took swipes at Geela, like she was up for grabs, or something. They tried to bite then wanted all of her, like they always did without gratitude or appreciation. But she wasn't up for grabs.

Who were these fat mobs gnawing at her? Vrucos and Coverdia intervened and, while piling them into heaps of carrion, eagle broke through, a portal of light shone, and Geela emerged with the shield and spear of a mother warrior in her hand. *Watch out* . . . crows thought. She had been tested and stood the proof and the crows fed her enemies to those languishing in the dungeons of old New York.

Slowly, patiently Agod restored Geela to her former self, the way only Agod's love could. After all, Geela was Agod's daughter and after years of service to the country she had returned home to White Tents and followed Agod.

Rising in the east, washing light flooded the land and everything she heard. The sun coursed one age after another and over the epochs, emboldened the shadows. Light shifted and fluttered, spilling immutable time.

The sun heard and backwards it went, its wily shadow agitating and cleverly, on summer wind or in mute-milk of winter sky it revealed, and Geela felt the change.

She joined with Ptarro and, along with Wreda Blord and many others in the Wilderness League, went to work for the top bosses, Vrucos and Coverdia. Geela was falcongentle to Agod now and sat tethered and hooded just outside Agod's tent. She had gone home: free like the wild river she flew, to where an uninterrupted sky kept Agod.

50

Chapter 17

Polar bears who lived at the North Pole, bears who binged and ate for six months and worked the extra weight off sleep-walking in winter while dreaming of seal, the ones who liked extreme light and darkness, those bears hosted a summit at the top of the world, roughly correlating with peak solar wind explosions.

Agod was sure the fate of the whole planet lay at the Arctic Circle, so Theocean, trickster and shaman to the way north, stole some sun from the South Pole just in time to throw a little extra light on this year's celebration. You see, intense auroral activity distorted radio waves and caused abnormal fluctuations in the earth's magnetic fields; power line and satellite transmittals deteriorated and interfered with government's ability to surveil and it was under this shield those in the boreal chose to discuss their business, and not be overheard.

The venue was a hunting camp used by Inuit engaged in subsistence hunting along the 66th parallel, and the bears got the place ready in grand, polar bear style. Carved spirit figures and contemplative creatures from myths, imitative of early Dorset culture, were placed about the region, arranged and posed in happy, playful scenes. Walrus, seal, bear and narwhal abounded in the region and took their places on ice floes, drifting and floating and bobbing on lyat gray approaching white. Fin-footed applause rang, hooting and cheering, flippers flapped and tails thrashed as aerial pirouette of pure joy spun in mid-air. A vagrant bovida from a nearby herd of muskox wandered into the event and was a little annoyed she hadn't been invited . . .

At night they camped in tents and ate fish. The locals prepared meals, all of it wild caught, in outdoor cooking pits, while overhead a warm, southerly, meridian air vaulted, lightly brushing the solar wind. Its amethyst ripples wagged dim lanterns, dragging purple, trailing, translucent streaks tacked to wavering, dark, rose-colored tails, their tips topped with yellow streaming stars – and the exploding light flared. Aurora circled the North Pole and her halos extended an ambiance that deeply affected Agod, and when Agod returned to White Tents after the celebration, Agod's heart was stout, Agod's spirit renewed and Agod carried critical intelligence to share with the League's compatriots in the south.

An ice bolt struck and a sudden, deadly chill fell over the assembled crowd. Theocean, shaman trickster and vanguard to the way north, stepped up to the podium. He was wearing sealskin—its soulskin meant a lot to him—it was his amulet, his mojo, and brought him great power.

He spent most of his days alone, in solitary paddle, making way aboard a kayak, circumventing the Circle, his inner magnetic force pulled by an invisible magnetosphere leading him through cold currents in icy water, allowing his energized particles to run wild and free, submitting to the power of magnetic fields that took him to the North Pole, and beyond. He had never been to Antarctica, but he'd sure like to go one day. In dreamtime he saw northern peoples there, with the polar bear, in a world seemingly turned upside down. From time to time he plied elsewhere, toward southern climes, and traveled along warmer, latitudinal lines, towards the equator, and Cancer and Capricorn, but this was rare for Theocean.

Those at the gathering examined critical issues in the Occident. Global warming was first and foremost on most people's minds and its impact on ice melt and the rate at which the height of tides was rising and flooding the land. The environmentalists, scientists, and sportsmen, after years of enmity, had wisely created a coalition, strengthening their position and voice, and after years of disagreement were finally on the same page – that is, the front page, top-fold, figuratively and literally speaking, expelling the corporatists from the conversation, along with the talking heads, hence the secrecy and less likelihood of eavesdropping and media spin.

Theocean, in prayerful reverence, raised his eyes over the crowd. "Every ten years or so, we meet to discuss critical issues occurring in the Occident," he announced. "The polar bears requested we begin with a report concerning global warming and its impact on ice melt and the rising heights of tides. Can you blame them?"

The crowd approved and nodding to one another murmured their consent then Theocean introduced speakers and moderated debates.

"The ice is melting at the North Pole, and fast, and soon the bears will be stranded," a spokeswoman for the group said. "Only animals who adapt will survive Albedo."

"Snow cover reflects a lot of radiation and open water absorbs it," Theocean agreed. "And Albedo has melted the snow so fast, changing white bear's life forever."

He cleared his throat. "The Arctic Ocean is the shortest route between North America and Russia," said Theocean, steering the conversation his way, "and as it has lost a lot of its permafrost it's open for sea travel most of the year."

"Governments fostered enmity between the countries . . . not their people. America, the government, must learn to share and get along with the rest of the world and not take more than their fair share, if they are to survive," warned Theocean.

"All people living along the Circle are my relatives and many of them are not North Americans . . . still . . . we all love one another . . ."

The sea route around the north of Canada and Alaska was nearly clear of ice now, and whales with dorsals could swim year-round. In the past, bowheads with no dorsals could easily travel under the ice but the other whales were denied passage when ice was present. It was different now.

Clipena was in the audience. She flew low over the group, squawking, her throat pouch flapping loosely. "Well, well, a coup de grâce? Severing the noggins off them talking heads . . . off their irreverent bodies? Their incessant week-long reporting and end-of-week discussions of their week-long reporting was too much, really; I say not too soon!"

She continued, "While media conducted itself as though it could persuade an entire population, and knead its minds, survivors abandoned technology and tracking devices and headed for the parklands."

"And the cherry on top . . . it's all over now . . . se acabó. We can think for ourselves, thank you very much."

She adopted a playful tone, pitching her message to the youngsters in the audience, "Any news from dethroned corporatists and decapitated talking heads is heretofore relegated to the obituary page."

Everyone laughed and cheered. They had managed to expel the corporatists from future talks, along with the talking, nodding heads and were feeling very good indeed.

"Let's eat. My people are here with food for all, treats from Blooming Flower, and elsewhere. C'mon, let's eat!" Clipena's white pelicans flew low and dropped fish, scallops, shrimp, oysters, and all kinds of other wild caught delicacies from their sacks. They emptied their pouches and everyone feasted. It was a delightful picnic at the North Pole and all the guests were well-fed while presenters made their speech.

The summit lasted for days and most discussions among the varying factions were peaceful. More remarkably, a coalition had been established among environmentalists, scientists, and sportsmen and its creation wildly encouraged everyone in the audience, bringing tears to their eyes. No more were the corporatists the leading force, no more the media prince in all the cities.

Theocean said, "Finally, after at least a century of enmity and conflict, they combined forces, and strengthened Agod's authority. Agod had hosted the peace talks in White Tents and what an extraordinary diplomatic accomplishment it was! After years our people are finally all on the same page, that is folks, the front page, top-fold!"

Caren Shilland, a sandhill crane, was in attendance with Fig Sherkin, a kingfisher and was Bow Darrel's emissary. She had much to say about abandoned fracking fissures. Wishtonwish was not here, nor Ptarro or Erhon Geren – they were marching with the ants; Clipena and her flock had seen them marching westward way while flying north on their way to the summit. Tossherrheim, Papel and Stoonman were crawling all over the continent, and someone in a latex suit printed with an American flag motif was skating on rollerblades on abandoned highways, all across America, someone no one seemed to know.

Ice blink reflected luminous on the horizon. Cotteeman showed himself and stood up, looking west then northwestward way and back at the assembly, then signaled. Agod saw him and knew it was time to go.

Agod stood with outstretched arms and the crowd went wild. Panthalassa powered Theocean's pounding pulse. Currents of electricity swirled around Agod. A hush fell over the assembly as Agod spoke Agod's mind.

"Glad tidings my friends. As you know, to the south, austral beings, Migla Fon and Lamon Fig, flamingo expatriates, want to come home, but not before Pahayokee is flushed clean. A great flood will come and it will rain for thirty months in the way south and the residue from sugar cane plantations and fertilizer toxins and plant feed will be flushed away in the big rain storms and the moving grass will rinse clean, once and for all. Will the remedy work and will the birds return from their Central American exile, from their banishment? I hope so . . . they are scheduled to navigate Florida Bay soon and I miss them. Please, let's pray together and bring them home," Agod somberly, and humbly, said.

Throughout the remaining summit hours other members of the League shared news and stories. Fireflies reported on natural resource levels around the continent and Theocean's way of life was shared with those who didn't know him. Ice was melting too fast, what could bears do? The deep, underground water inside the fracking shafts must be forever cleaned and then cleaned some more.

Delegates and personnel assigned to track developments around the continent continued to read out reports. More serious discussions followed: fracking and its impact on under-the-ground water quality were of paramount importance; the health of first growth forests lamented. True, Sequoia and Greylock had somehow managed to thrive with their old growths, with their bee colonies and Happy People, and Agod wanted it to remain that way.

Agod was the summit's most revered guest, but Agod's knights weren't here with Agod. Living above the bogs and waterways of central Canada and beyond, down and away, in areas accessible only by air, as did others in Canada's north, all members of the same Wilderness League, working towards the same common goals, Vrucos and Coverdia were occupied, guiding Geela, Agod's daughter, safely home to White Tents.

Chapter 18

The rain began. There was no wind at all and the rain fell straight. The ants watched as it pelted the surface of the dry road, and then as the earth floated loose of the road and changed to mud in streams and rivulets. Sobs swept over them but they sucked in their cries and, although many were drowning, with one voice sang, *Oh, Agod, we are glad, and grateful, oh my Agod, we are so thankful for the rain.*

Crow glided silently over the road and through the rain watched the ant's joy manifest through tears and suffering, but the crow, like the deer, said nothing, did not think of past or future, but was present, and witness.

Ahead, far into the mountains, on a high snowy range, the marching ants saw the blinking, billowing snows of White Tents, its pitched, luminous sheets humming and snapping like laundry linens on a breeze. The glaciers had all melted, and along its windy slopes water shed east and west. Geela was eagle and lived here in White Tents. She was falcongentle, and kept tethered just outside Agod's tent.

Geela's life's path, the soul around which her body developed and grew, changed course along its way. A trail opened and washed, eastern light shined – the light she heard. Vaulting east to west, the shadow of day shifted and scurried on the wind and in evening shrouded the city in dreamtime. Reposed in twilight, western voice fell in White Tents and the city somnambulated, its white sails flapping high on a Wyoming range, fluttering, far away from the ant colonies, and yet the light was heard.

Vrucos and Coverida had found her living like a tramp in a subway hovel. Over great disagreement and much dissent, she had been cast out by Treasury and let alone to vanquish and die. Agod had sent the crows to fetch her—she was still alive—and bring her back home.

Ptarro and many others were on their way to White Tents too and while Geela greeted the guests as they arrived, she pondered what the chiefs from the north, Vrucos and Coverdia, recently told her.

'Water conservation is not enough for the survival of western agricultural states. You must convene a meeting to strategize on policy to pipe water from the eastern great lakes and large rivers to drought-stricken lands west of here.'

Geela closed her eyes. On the screens of her lids shape-shifting faces revealed and millennia receded to a primeval land when faces were chiseled according to tribe. Once genetics—jaw lines and cheek bones . . . one of mine, one of yours—and inflections, the way lips curled around words and pronounced phonetics, defined tribes. Not anymore. Today mixed groups of remainders and reminders of a former modern epoch populated clans. Some lived in boats on the Great Lakes, while others pitched tents along the divide; a few humans clung to the great sequoias in the west and glade dwellers hid in mangroves, too afraid to fly about as they once did. Some lived in beehives while others drifted with turtles on the Sargasso Sea, clinging to seaweed, floating along on calm waters . . . waiting.

All over the North American continent, today, Geela thought, *boundaries are determined by ecosystems, the country had become an immense parkland made up of diverse communities: tent cities, tree huts, boat houses, beehives and underground shelters . . . all modeled after a national park system; districts were arranged by task and were very democratic places.*

Clouds arranged for a dozen or more windward instruments and filled the airspace; staves of music drifted downward . . . their notes hand-ruled by Agod. A high wind trilled a stanza or two while birds sang color in lower pitch. Light paused and animals whistled legato amidst whirling, swirling strokes of shade.

With compact and puff in hand, Geela palmed pink powder on her wizened face. Residents in White Tents saw Agod in her face and imagined she was an eagle descended from an aerie placed high on a mountain cliff in the clouds. Still, she would wear her wind-burned skin blushes this evening, along with lipstick and crepe to the conference, a wind and sun blush, bloomed earlier in the day.

She fingered her earrings for a moment then slipped them onto her ears. Nearby, in the plaza, Agod played at chess with some of the men, while dappled sunlight filtered through blousy, bobbing branches of mulberry tree where refracting light captured and binded pink and red, and a chromolithograph printed crazy, swirling, fornicating color about their chairs. Looking at them, then back again at her face in the mirror, still fingering the hammered earrings, again at the men and back at her face, she was reminded of Wreda Blord. Never was there a woman so bent on getting under another woman's feathers than Wreda Blord. *She will be here this evening, Wreda will be here and I'll ask her why the mission at Maplewood failed . . . why she and Ptarro weren't able to stop the Chinese.*

And what do you know? Just as Geela was thinking all this, Wreda strolled in from off a path leading to the square where the men and Agod were playing chess. She wore a stole capelet of moss, trimmed to fit her shoulders, it hung lushly off her heavy frame and pinecones dangled from its fringed edge. Wreda was barred owl and silversmith by trade and the blossom bursts worn by Geela were crafted by Wreda, presented as a gift one evening over dinner, many years ago . . .

Wreda's artifice was her aloof psychology, and she used it, cleverly, to penetrate a person's brain. This was her power. *Penmanship, a man's handwriting, odd, how unusual, to be aroused by a man's penmanship . . .* Wreda had said just this to Geela one evening over dinner and in a flirtatious mood referred to a letter, posted by Ptarro, regarding intelligence at Maplewood. Geela suspected Wreda was up to something, a foil perhaps, that fat overweight owl, who ran faster than she flew, wanted her post perhaps, to be falcongentle to Agod . . . or maybe she just wanted Ptarro?

No, Geela thought, *Wreda is a young soul and careless, finding her way, clever, of course, but still finding her way* and dropped it. In dim of twilight more was seen and less was heard.

The children of White Tents played and caught buzzing insects in glass jars: first trapping, then dropping them into the tight space for a closer look. Nearby a cat licked its paws and considered the scene, performing an ablution, its cat wash. *Cider, apple pie, and ice cream for supper tonight,* the children shouted. Apples could be cultivated without pesticide or insecticide here. At certain altitudes, fruit killing bugs didn't thrive and White Tents was one of them. *Yum.*

Greet Withe stood just inside the door to Agod's tent looking out over the yard into a wooded lot. Caren Shilland shifted towards the door and stood next to her, out of curiosity. *What was Greet looking at? What was so fascinating and at this time of day?*

The others were inside, in another room, talking quietly amongst themselves. Greet peered through the top half of the back door—it was covered in screen—past the stoop, and into the yard where three very alert baby owls stared back from the safety of a nest buttressed in a crook of a nearby tree. Caren looked too and watched as mom tried to feed them, tried to force pieces of fresh, torn kill down their throats but the owlets were curious and, squirming, refused the food she forced. Greet turned away.

Caren asked, "Who are they?"

Greet, having left the door, was already busy painting her toenails. Yellow was her favorite color and in summer, with sandals and other open-toed shoes, and the sheer black hose she loved to wear, she kept her pedicure up.

"They are our relatives," said Greet, wriggling and flexing her freshly painted toes.

"They communicate without words, just like in dreamtime. This is dreamtime, Caren, where everything gets set up. Their young spirit evokes . . . evokes what Caren? They want you to see past the limitations of your intelligence. Who are they? I think

57

they are messengers from the migrant workers and the Wilderness League will need help from them soon."

Greet was an emissary for Geela. She lurked along the Rio Grande and patrolled the riverbed and counted and tagged Jumping Beans for census reports. The Beans lived Another Way and fascinated everyone in the Wilderness League; living mostly in Mexico, they loved to travel and like the little moths, the frijoles saltarines, they inhabited the beans and lay eggs in their pods and when the time was right they changed shape and jumped all around the Americas, north and south, east and west − it was their nature.

Greet made many trips between Rio and White Tents. She packed lightly for her journeys, often storing her lunch in a bug box − some days it was a mouse. Bug boxes were fashionable in Greet's world and she had several. (She had a box to complement nearly every outfit she wore and changed them as often as another woman might change the color of her lipstick or nail polish, or her clothes. Greet was fickle that way.)

Greet Withe, the crazy lady with the yellow toenails, had arrived in White Tents. She wore black stockings, and white plumes on her hat, her dress was embroidered with fresh water pearls and satiny down. She carried a bug box and had packed her lunch in it, alive. One aspect of the box was magnified to scare her enemies, another side fixed with a latch for easy access. In it she kept her companion of the day and today would have it for lunch.

She loved the way a rainy day made her feel and while inside the rhythms the rain brought she'd splash and wade and as the soft pellets hit her and she drew water with the forward movement of her legs, she would think about American women. At one time American women were much admired around the globe, but not anymore: they had lost their power when they forsook beauty. Greet sighed . . . another piece of soul that must be retrieved.

Greet's arrival had broken the ice. Her long legs and yellow toenails, black stockings and bug box were good topics for conversation and she loved the attention. She worked hard to cultivate an image of allurement, seduction was a big part of her power, and there were so many to seduce.

The bug in her box was safe, for the time being, but was horrified as it listened to people in the room discussing insect farming, raising bugs for an inexpensive protein food, for human consumption and a quick snack.

"Yes, a group of women in Central Valley created a line of snack food called Bug Bites. They freeze-dry the little buggers and flavor them with salt or sugar."

"Greet over there," said Wreda laughing, tossing her head towards the door, "eats her food alive, but there are others who just can't stomach that sort of thing."

All the guests had arrived and were swapping stories. Ptarro was sitting in a sunny spot when Greet joined them; he was talking about the ant colony and the first time he saw it. He described the mission at Maplewood too. Someone was sent to fetch Agod. Ptarro continued shape-shifting his tales though he did not understand how he did it, or why, and Wreda listened while he told story, then, after a nap, she told everyone there about the House Boat People who were living coyote way.

There were a lot of youngsters in the room with eager minds and the adults told story to inform them, but in a playful manner, so the children could better understand the events that shaped what the country had become: playful accounts of serious events, the characters extraordinary. The narrators changed from one story to the next, first Ptarro then Bow Darrel, next Wishtonwish and Fig Sherkin, everyone in attendance who had pledged to help Agod and Geela save the Wilderness League from greedy, destructive human activity. Caren Shilland and Erhon Geren were there too . . . they were younger than the others and had much to learn and had not heard any of the stories shared that afternoon.

Happy People were there with their attendant sequoias and sat fortified in ramparts in the good old trees; Greylock was there too, with the old growth spruce, but they remained outside the perimeter of White Tents. They were good soldiers and great warriors and runners were sent to relay what was discussed under the tent. Children scampered up and over, climbing and playing on the great trees, while the adults discussed how to fix the continent.

The sun slipped over the mountains. Agod listened while Wreda Blord finished describing the barnyard scene at Maplewood, then Agod rose and greeted the group.

"Geela has returned and I am so very happy, and proud. But government exploited her and tossed her out into the streets and it's time to repair the mess it has made."

Geela stood and asked, "Can we save the animals, and the land, and surviving people, the ones who embrace Another Way, and the Sun Life too? Or are we too late? Have the failure of globalism and the West's version of capitalism destroyed America forever, its land, its people, its culture, and its wildlife with its never ending consumption and greed?"

"There is a severe water shortage in the agricultural districts to the west and the ants will have to haul water from Middle River to California. Ptarro will lead them," Agod continued.

Geela interrupted, "Wreda, why weren't you and Ptarro able to stop the sale of Maplewood to the Chinese?"

Wreda looked over at Ptarro. He dropped his head. Agod waited for Wreda to respond.

"It wasn't anything we did Geela . . . honest. There were so many of them chickens, there was nothing we could do . . . they had so much mock and so much credit that government allowed our food supply to be sold out from under us. Now two billion people in Asia eat first and we get the scraps."

Americans, overtime, had become casual and aloof, imperious really, and like all aristocrats before them believed they ought to own the future and immortality too. In dishabille a new aristocracy emerged, dressed casually like slobs. But their sense of entitlement bred insouciance and, when mock failed, perpetual indebtedness from beyond the grave drove them to despair.

For years League members did their wash once a week and hung it out to dry, folding and patting their piles into baskets later in the day . . . fresh-washed laundry for the coming week. Like those in the Wilderness League government did its wash too and, piled high in laundry baskets, mock that grew on trees stretched as high as the sky.

But who paid the laundry bill? And who got the credit?

The bill came in the electronic mail, late one electric night; while everyone lie sleeping debt piled on the people, just before mock died. People got the bill, but then all credit died and perpetual indebtedness drove people to despair.

No cash, no gas, and no pensions either – the system had collapsed. No mock for fuel or food or heat and with groceries shuttered, banks closed, plastic didn't work; no banker could find a remedy or solution, and survivors scattered into parkland tribes.

Agod glanced around at the guests under the tent. "The ants are marching westward way and have only stopped so Ptarro could attend this summit."

"Wishtonwish and his crew will soon commence to clean contaminated groundwater of toxins. Wishtonwish began his service in the Great Plains in a place called *la prairie* and is prairie dog . . . and . . . in case any of you were wondering, his name is a native imitative of a prairie dog's cry. He lurks in the pulse, nerves, arteries and veins of the planet, in an underground world of abandoned fracking and sand tar extraction, where oil and gas once swelled."

"In tunnels and trenches under the boreal forests near the Athabasca River in Canada, under public lands in Utah and along the Orinoco River basin in Venezuela and anywhere oil sands were extracted or shale was fractured by high pressure drilling techniques, you will find Wishtonwish. Although these processes caused the earth to heat up, and fast, industry and government were only focused on any immediate economic benefits . . . just another example of choking the earth to make a few bucks."

"Over time I've seen very few signs of intelligence amongst the planet's big players. And lately if anyone knew better and protested, well, government had a store of everyone's metadata and could easily manipulate it and make a case against protesters and destroy anyone who tried to interfere with its agendas."

Agod paused. "That's over now, finished, but it nearly destroyed us all. People never did anything so right as to abandon technology."

"Wishtonwish is part of the Wilderness League and reports to mid-continent chief, Caren Shilland and, oh, Caren, she is sandhill crane."

"Erhon Geren is a garbage heap specialist and is chronicling the history of America's wastrels by examining its trash piles. His commentary is illuminating and I recommend it for reading. What was thrown out ought to embarrass people . . . really . . . consumptive heaps of trash. But underground eco-terrorists are not wastrels and recycle everything people throw out."

Agod inhaled a big breath. "So many of us have had special relationships with particular parts of the country and particular food sources for so very long now and we might think we are not adaptable, like a highly specialized plant, perhaps, that can only be pollinated by a specific insect, and can only live a certain way. But this is not true. We must all learn to adapt in ways we have never imagined, or die."

"And what an opportunity; survivors are looking to us to lead the way. We must apply all our skills to the problems at hand, with a creativity that will awe and amaze all who observe us . . . model it . . . for the survivors, so this will never happen again."

"Many have learned to adapt, and these are the ones who will survive. Some of you will think this can't be done but listen to what I have to say."

"Some flowers have highly evolved structures through which only one species can navigate but they know how to mimic females of a particular insect and fool the male into copulation. For instance, a bucket flower can attract a male bee with its sweet scent. The bees fall into the upside-down bell-shaped flower that's filled with a thick, sticky liquid but their wings become so drenched and heavy with the solution they almost drown, and the bee is forced to escape by crawling back out rather than flying. But the male crawls out of that bucket orchid with two packets of pollen deposited on his back, not one."

"I like that," laughed Wreda.

Agod continued, "Cultivate fascinating, complex, extraordinary relationships with them, the ones who embrace Another Way . . . it is our last chance. Intoxicate them. This must never happen again. Nature is so full of diversity and dexterity we ought to be able to succeed."

"Yes, greed nearly wiped the planet out, all of it, killing and destroying all. And yes, while it's true, some only got interested in survival when they realized they were next to be vanquished, the ones who figured it out have scattered into parkland tribes – they are the survivors and want to cooperate with us."

"Sound familiar?" asked Ptarro sarcastically.

Agod looked past the setting sun and with a solemn voice, struggled to find the words to explain to the adults in the room what Agod thought would be the most difficult concept for them to wrap their minds around. Agod depended on Geela for help.

"Wreda's surveillance, and the intelligence she gleaned, allowed all of us—me, you, Greet here, and all the rest in the Wilderness League—to understand how far gone the country had become. Believe me when I say this: it was the ascendency of an elite by way of the rapid electronic transmission of mock that heralded the end for America."

"It may be difficult to wrap your heads around this but the West's version of capitalism and its aberrant and warped creation of mock signaled the beginning of its decline. Their motto *'let there be electronic money, though the whole world perish'* was a dangerous one."

"Let's hope nothing like this ever happens again. Meanwhile, what can we do to restore the continent to health?"

Geela said, "Mock stole the future. You see, money is mock and mock is money. The land and minerals and water and food and timber, all of it, was securitized – then repackaged and loaned upon the American people."

"Excessive greed and consumption, a desire to own the whole world, inspired the elites to expropriate the world's assets and securitize them all. They are greedy fat ducks."

"How was it we were forced to sell our country out from under us, to the whole world? Others had their countries, and we had ours."

Geela was on a rant. "It wasn't government's to give away or sell but they did it anyway, and arbitraged our standard of living. Government mortgaged our prosperity, and gave us the debt. It expropriated our labor and wealth, and to pay for it set us all on a road to serfdom."

"Why, government ought to have returned the land to its rightful owners, don't you think, give it back to the first people and the wild creatures if they were feeling so magnanimous? Who do they think they are?" asked Ptarro.

Greet opined, in a serious tone not particularly characteristic of her. "You see, for years Americans took more than their fair share from the world's offertory plate and we animals and birds, we knew it, we could see it coming. You never, ever take more than you need . . . less is so much, much more."

She shifted, then crossed her legs. Her long, loose, lanky pins were veiled in black and her white plumed hat had been placed carefully on the table nearby. The dress she wore, what a delight! A shiny, satiny, embroidered frock of fresh water pearl, bugle bead and downy goose feather draped over her elegant frame and on her arm hung a bug box, which she used for a handbag, and inside it her companion-of-the-week, a pink-spotted hummingbird moth.

Her well-manicured, yellow-painted toenails pushed through the tiny peeps of her pretty shoes that were dangling and hooked on her feet. The moth pointed and opened its bill and whipping its tongue tickled the tip of Greet's wing, playfully pulling at a feather.

Greet quickly turned and snapped, "Stop it."

It shrank back into the box. Wishtonwish was wide-eyed. *Wow,* he thought. He had never seen a bug do that before.

"Consumption fired American-styled capitalism, not conservation. Consumptive competition in a world of dwindling resources . . . how stupid was that? Enough is never good enough for greedy people. They ate way too much and are *so* screwed now because when greedy corporatists control governments, people starve. I mean . . . those who can't plant a garden will starve. Less is more, so much, much more," Greet's voice trailed off.

"Corporatists and governments and bankers arbitraged the American standard of living. Do you understand this? And by securitizing the future, took possession of it, and possession of most Americans, trading them up and trading them off, and collateralized or not, all the hedgerows in the world couldn't protect them from what came next."

Geela agreed. "Yes, and that's why I'm out of a job."

She got up and twirled about the room. "How do you like America's fancy skirtwork? Do-si-do! Bow-to-your partner! How do you like it? Her fancy skirtwork? Well, her shadow partners stole the lead, didn't they? Wrong turn thar!"

Greet was exasperated. "Oh, sit down Geela. We get it, but it's so darn boring. America slouched and her people were chained to a road of serfdom."

Greet cried out, "I can't keep it all straight! I'd rather watch a spider sleep than clutter my mind with this crap!"

"What in the world, my flappin' wings. I didn't get it till just now. Them darned central bankers . . . them darned bankers, what kinda mess have they got us into?" cried Ptarro.

Geela asked, "So, what do we do now?"

Agod said, "For the early North American Indian, ambush was a successful hunting technique. They would set up near a watering hole and wait for thirsty animals to come and get a drink. Then they'd sneak up until they were close enough to throw a spear and once the animal was wounded the hunters would follow, harassing it until it died."

"And . . . that's what we will do," said Agod.

Agod finished, "The issue of food supply is tantamount, of course, but right now the bears' fate is the most important task to tackle. Global temperatures must come down so the white bears can stay at the North Pole. I understand this will not happen overnight, so, in the meantime I suggest all of you get rid of any remaining tracking devices - cell phones, anything that can trace your moves. We don't want the greedy ones thwarting your efforts and preventing your success."

Chapter 19

The phone rang. It was Nojá from Los Angeles. She did all her talking in dreamtime and when she was awake had nothing to say, ever. She was asleep when she called.

Nojá was curious, blond and short, with long arms and fairly thin legs, varicosed and veined. Her slender hips and broad shoulders gave her a masculine appearance. The bleach in her blond slumped into a filmy mop and the fat on her upper back hung over her bra straps in small bunches that looked like little sacks of flour; she was over forty, closer to fifty.

Yes, she was blond, alright, but past all the fun. It was Valentine's Day and her man was inside a bottle, swimming in his sea of love and, every so often . . . Nojá was saying . . . he'd resurface . . .

"I mean he's inside that bottle, girls, tongue lickin' laps round its rim, past infinite void, and after a while settles lifelessly at bottom. There, in its depths, the pressure of submersion forces him back again towards the lighter density of alcohol and occasionally he pops through the bottle neck, where the cork goes, bobbing like he's in a swimming pool or something and with his elbows props himself up and holds on, takes a quick look around, dries out for minute, flirts with a beautiful woman sitting on a chaise . . . or whatever . . . then he lets go and slips back inside the bottle."

Today Nojá was dreaming about insects. She had been eating them all summer long because the valleys were too dry to support any kind of farming. They couldn't really afford to buy them, they were too expensive for their budget but trash can picking simply wasn't yielding what it ought to, and she was hungry. Her husband was drinking again, and way too much since his dogs last run off.

Nojá sighed. They had just come from Central Valley and as they traveled through fields and fields of winter crops Jumping Beans were bent over their work, every inch of their bodies covered with colorful clothing, even their faces. They kept the sun off the best they could, draping tee shirts over their heads or tucking them under a visor cap; out in the field tee shirts were worn under caps and hats and tucked inside collars legionnaire-style to keep the sun off their necks and large duckbill flaps extended prominently in extreme conditions.

In the heat, all day long, short men and short women carried baskets close to the ground. Trucks transported them from one field to another and heavy equipment moved their harvest from bumper to hopper.

"Americans thought they could give equal access to the whole world and tried to make the country available to everyone which, it turns out, was a ridiculous idea. We got nothing to give away anymore, the future has been sold out from under us. Nothing, besides, oughtn't America be returned to those from whom it was taken, rather than given away?" Nojá mused.

"I watched a bicyclist emerge from a tomato field," Nojá said, "a man from a refugee camp – small, dark-skinned, with sweaty clothes and sweaty skin . . . always sweaty, always smelly, after a wash his clothes still stinky and stained. I could say those people never looked clean but then Americans had to have their cake and eat it too, didn't they? And eat it too is what they did. Holy smoke, they ate all of theirs and yours and mine. My grandchildren are paying the bill for things my grandmother needed forty years ago and couldn't afford."

"The way back was along a flat, straight strip of asphalt through corporate-sized tomato fields, and ghettoes . . . migrant ghettoes and refugee camps. The road ran alongside a canal that had been dug years earlier and the canal ran with this straight, flat strip of asphalt. It was dark and on the night road a chock full bus of workers sped by, past the big retail stores directly to an off-site store owned by who knows who, charging way too much for who knows what, way too much. A recurring theme, and now the exploitation of field hands has extended to the larger population of American serfs, and those people weren't allowed out of sight, either, that is, till they smartened up and abandon technology."

Nojá stopped dreaming and hung up. Lithil said, "We ought to take this book to Nojá in Los Angeles, she's come undone. Bring the book to her, it tells all about the parkland way. Maybe Nojá and her husband ought to move and live with the survivors in the parklands who pursue Another Way, the Sun Life way."

Lithil blurted out, "Let's share the book with the whole world."

Occo obliged. "Yes, Lithil, we will stop time, change shape and fly to Los Angeles and help Nojá."

They put the magic book down. Dream draped time and lifted Occo then Lithil from off their chairs and an everyday life that was guided by plant intelligence and daylight, emerged through a visionary pathway and before Lithil's eyes Occo changed shape and became Greet Withe, and Lithil watched her own body as she metamorphosed into Wreda Blord. They flew to California where the ants might succeed with irrigation efforts and where one day crops might grow and the Hollywood rich might resume their gorging and be opinionated again and, maybe, throw away some scraps so people like Nojá might eat . . . so people like Nojá may have crumbs again.

Tossherrheim was listening in on Nojá's call to Occo and was really, really mad.

Chapter 20

Straining under heavy loads, the ants sang simple tempos of rhythmically batched blue notes and shouted lamentingly sad work chants like *Oh, Baby, Oh* and *Carry Me Along* as they dragged bulky hose over one rise then another and followed with a refrain *Heave-Ho, Whoa Boys, Heave-Ho* when the work shifted downhill.

The ants in the ranks were in their ant-way talking about a girl farmer in Central Valley who developed a new snack food called Bug Bites. Bugs Bite? No, silly, Bug Bites. This was not enough to sustain a people the ants thought. It repulsed them, but what could they do? They were a voiceless mass, but otherwise well-treated. The ants were struggling to bring water to areas where it was needed and wonder if they won't all be killed trying.

In the heat of the day the captain wanted a word, and ducking and skulking, edged away from the swarming ranks. At the fore he sidled in and, adopting Ptarro's cadence, fell in longside the old bird as he pushed westward way. Pilson Bloo was flying over their heads—low, languid and lazy—and she wanted in on the walkie-talkie.

Ptarro cranked his stiff neck to look at her and asked, "How was your flight? Pleasant?"

She fluttered and replied, "Sí, tranquilo." Pilson loved to show off her bilingual skills.

Ptarro wiped his brow. His eyes wandered over Erhon Geren's profile, anticipating his mood.

Ptarro whistled, "Man, oh man, Erhon, oh, my captain, oh, we got a real long way to go! Well, never mind that. Hey, what do you think of that Bow? You seen him? He's something else ain't he? He lives in an ancient sequoia on Vancouver Island."

Geren replied, "That's what I heard. Bow's an owl, ain't he? People live up there, I'm told, in those sequoias, way up there in the Canada north."

Until recently Pilson had never heard of people who clung to trees and wandered about at trees' pleasure and her pink mind and pink feathers were blown away forever.

Pilson's flight undulated as she croaked, "... *khuh* ... *khuh* ... *khuh* ... they got an awesome way of getting around, those men, women, even the kids. They cling to them enormous blessed trees, yes sir, those trunks a-swaying and a-perambulating, in a darn peculiar way too, te lo juro por Dios, with those people astride."

"Bow straddles and steers those great tree trunks and when they walk through the forest everything in their path gets out of their way and gives a wide berth. Heck, those sequoias are smart," Ptarro cried as he slapped Erhon on the back.

Pilson flew closer to Ptarro and playfully snatched the cap from his head. "They organized a ride-sharing network for all those human beings in Vancouver. Rico o pobre, they get a ride. Oh my, what an extraordinary intelligence is working through their roots," she said as she dropped Ptarro's hat on Erhon's head.

"That red-head hangs around the Happy People, the one who is always singing. His horse sings too, you know. I heard them once . . . singing."

"Bow knows him. They work together sometimes."

"The massive wood roams freely about the country and, taken in stride, the tree dwellers wander about at the pleasure of the sequoia."

The trees had many limbs and could hug and carry as many survivors as found their way. Then Ptarro spoke softly, reverentially, almost to himself, "How wondrous really! Bow seen all this in a dream, he told me so himself. He traveled a far way to be with those sequoias, and all those Happy People who live there in the Canada north."

As they marched along, the troops made slow progress. The captain fell out of step but quickly skipped a stride, marking time again with Ptarro. The youngster was from Platte and had volunteered for the mission. It was a special operation and as he was green heron his rank demanded that he march with the company of fire ants all the way to California.

Erhon collaborated with Wishtonwish in the tunnels and trenches of *la prairie* and Caren Shilland oversaw their operations. Wishtonwish was there too, with the ants. He brought up the rear, a vulnerable flank, in prairie dog fashion, and didn't miss an opportunity to forage and feed along the way. When not on special operations duty, Wishtonwish and Erhon monitored the effects of underground fracking and sand tar extraction on the pulse, nerves, arteries and veins of the continent and southern Americas. They were members of an underground network and their task was to watch the frackers, the dirty, vilified frackers, and to report back to the mid-continent chief, Caren Shilland.

Pilson Bloo liked to be where the action was. She was roseate spoonbill and flew reconnoiter for the allies. Her base was in Blooming Flower. The state was one big agricultural district, but unlike California, had a surfeit of water for its irrigation needs.

Florida was hit hard by climate change. Extraordinary tides had breached the coastal coral that defended the peninsula but rosenskedstork, her spatula rosée, resided in a fluid place, and it was no matter. Pilson lived in a silk tent, a tent woven with threads spun by her caterpillar friends, and her chief vanity was her pink feathers.

In the evening she camped under a lunar lamp. When green faded to moonlight and breeze puffed lightly, whitewash drained its cast and, erasing dimension, the branches and leaves and flowers and hanging fruit danced a mime of silhouette on tent's silk drape. Shadows leapt and illuminated the screen and while damp vapors lifted off the earth and permeated the hut she, just before sleep, croaked a yawn and a sibilant slide scraped a sound like a rake dragged over slate, and a scary, eerie, primeval lonesome sounded the night.

Palm fronds, mahogany leaves, and live oak implicated. Tropical plants imprinted the silk tent walls with shadow and when wind blew the tent walls shook and filled with air and although it was anchored seemed to pick up and fly while she slept.

Evenings were blustery. They excited and stimulated her and she slept very little and during the night when the tent plopped down in another place and time, she was awake. Anyone alive, anyone living outside on the planet and working outside on the planet, making his or her living hunting or fishing or growing, understood nature but others, *oh my Agod,* camping alongside her or living in the refugee camps outside Miamia, didn't know enough to obey their dreams.

Survivors were returning to the rhythms of the natural world and this narrative was continent-wide, indigenous to the northern Americas and the southern Americas, but it amazed Pilson how far so many others had drifted, how atrophied their senses had become. The wind and its force and energy sustained life. Bugs and birds were fragile, terribly fragile, but couldn't exist without the wind and here in Blooming Flower she wasn't seeing a lot of either birds or bugs. She knew she must get up and leave in the morning, and help Ptarro.

Ptarro sighed and thought, *Back in the saddle again.* He knew his sleepy, nodding fawn-lily furlough days were over, at least for a while. Oh, how he loved to sleep away his days in a hammock, strung over the twinkling lights of a riverbed. But the enormous continental task of watering vegetables and grains and orchards of fruits and nuts lay ahead. It had been assigned to the fire ants and he understood the solemnity, the responsibility of it all: a nation's food supply was in danger. As there were no fires or flames in canyons or forests to fight, and no funeral pyres to tend, the ants were conscripted for irrigation duty in Central Valley and in arroyos surrounding the slowly evaporating Colorado.

When they reached the Colorado the ants made a chain of themselves by interlocking their legs and stretched, like many ladders, across the wide and dangerous river; crocheted and macramed into a bridge-like net, similar to a rope bridge but not hung, simply suspended on the surface tension of the water, they spread out on the very large and powerful river and rocked and rolled in fast-flowing white-water current, up and over white caps and back down again, not a sleepy black-water with deep, slow moving channels but a treacherous, rapidly-flowing, tumultuous current and the queen and her young managed to stay safe and dry. Worker ants carefully guided her and the youngsters and somehow they got across the Colorado.

It was a marvelous thing to see and so neat that Ptarro and company jumped up and down and shouted with pure joy at the sight of their intelligence. Somehow the front line began to reach the other side and the ants disentangled and disembarked and, unloading like a ferry, its passengers stepped off and resumed their march, dragging hose.

Chapter 21

All last night it rained, like spider webs it rained, and like spiders weaving webs the rain made spongy contact with the organic, decomposing earth and weaving webs like spiders, retreated. Its gauze stretched and pulled but still adhered to the earth and rain yawned while spider recalculated.

Blooming Flower separated from the continent and was adrift now, and a moat of shallow, shark-infested saltwater surrounded, creeping with crocodiles. The flamingoes knew where to step though and picked their way around the predators . . . after everything, after it all, this was easy stuff for flamingo.

Florida Bay beckoned and enticed. A glittering attitude of sparkling azure drew latitudinal lines that floated on wavy space, then floated keys and floated birds. Beset with jewels and looking south the bay's brown grass waved a scintillating blend of visible and invisible light and flamingo appeared, enchanted.

Jewel sparkled and magic sighed. Out in front Migla Fon and Lamon Fig waded, leading snaking, aerial whips of flamingo wending down, whirling down, winding down towards the bay from a heaven in the sky. Then the ground nesters, millions of them danced on lanky pins, walking this way then that, stopping, occasionally, to bouse. Awkward shapes of pelican floated overhead, others waddled over to greet them. White wood stork clicked their bills like chop sticks and, enthusiastically nodding, hailed flamingo.

In the middle of it all, creepy men crawled along on their bellies like snakes; men with shotguns, with brush strapped to their backs hid and waited. In ambush they jumped up and fired as the whippets approached the earth and shot and shot indiscriminately for sport and pink feathers. Here, now gone, in the millions, just for the heck of it. Oh, wildlife refuges had been squeezed in and cordoned off, but in amongst slick roadways overflowing with fast automobiles traveling at great speeds, carrying over-consuming people, rushing towards fast food and amusement and, yes, a few deer had managed to survive, but they were locked in behind a fence . . . along with panther.

Corporations had moved fast to control fresh water on the planet, and then securitized it. Securitized it all and made an asset class out of it, along with seeds and the oceans, and all the fishes in the oceans. The Wilderness League really didn't understand how, but the earth's elements had all been securitized.

Panthalassa had long caressed Pangaea, and loved her. Pangaea drifted and overtime it journeyed westward and eastward and northward and southward but Blooming Flower was still part of Africa, Pahayokee a piece of Africa, and it felt right under their feet, so Migla Fon and her lover Lamon Fig led the flamingoes back home to here and Migla and Lamon returned. They waded towards Pahayokee, towards the moving grass and they had come a long way . . . all the way from Africa.

Meanwhile, sea turtles spun off their round and round orbit and returned to shore and searched for survivors along the mangrove coast – survivors who hid and waited for turtle to come and take them away, take them to Sargasso for a respite and reprieve. Pilson Bloo hailed from here and knew well the genocide in the breeding grounds that was killing bird and turtle populations, rendering them infertile. Nevertheless turtle worked hard to rescue people fleeing corporatists and a lifetime of serfdom. Survivors hid in the mangroves and turtle power brought them to the gyre, to turtle-run Sargasso for a retreat, and to heal.

Sea turtle moved steadily underwater and stroking their front leg-flaps, pulled the way men and women pulled when rowing a boat and, floating soundlessly, glided forward with survivors on their backs. In the water, day and night, turtles using their natural oars brought survivors to the gyre where they remained on turtle's back living a sargassian life, and round and round outside political boundaries, some began to think and plot how to save the continent. Oh, Tossherrheim might pursue, but somehow, you had better believe, turtle won the race.

Flamingo walked on tip-toes across Florida Bay, stopping along the way at mangrove islands to rest, and to shelter. The bay was a shallow place, shallow enough to walk across and flamingo watched as turtles with people on their backs rose and stretched and popped their heads through the bay's surface for a gulp of air. Survivors held on tightly and breathed like turtle did. Underwater it rained and turtle, turning out all light, buried their heads in seagrass for a while and rested. Exotic fish flew and swam about, in and out of turtle wakes, and at rocks turtles cleaned themselves and the people were amazed. Theocean visited this gyre from time to time and got away from the cold. He liked the trance-like state of the round and round and could see his power more clearly outside the white noise of political boundaries.

Over in Miamia, night rose and lit up the sky. Aromas wafted from the kitchens of restaurants and music winded and wandered around street corners. People cleaned up and strolled and paraded about, fancy rich people gazing at storefront window displays, people who came for a glimpse of America in its trendy, glamourous, merchandising days, yearning for a sniff. The streets were showcase, well, because the museums were closed, and the masterworks gone.

In Miamia, a little bit of a lot of worlds were scattered throughout its streets, foreign markets on main streets in an American city. Not a field picker's farmer's market but a greedy, gluttonous, food hunter's venue. Smoked fish, salmon, whole and wild-caught; grouper, snow crab legs, stone crab, red king crab, Key West pink shrimp, lobster, squid tubes and tentacles; live black mussels, little neck clams, oysters, sea scallops and holy mackerel; fresh ground almond butter, fresh ground peanut butter, ground chocolate, fresh ground honey-roasted almond butter and make your own granola. The smells were incredible, aromas found in European deli markets: French markets, Italian markets, German ones too; sumptuous wines and cheeses, milk products, organic milk, olives; Italian sodas and any kind of imagined artisan domestic or imported beer, micro brews and fresh pasta, though in reality good food had been priced out of reach of most people and became a showcase, and the unwanted, unneeded, and unnecessary looked on and salivated.

A young woman was hunched over a canvas on a sidewalk in the shade of a banyan tree. She was painting moody scenes and, like highwaymen before her, painted good stuff. Rags hung from her easel and were dabbed with many colors of pigment. She wiped her brush on the back of her shirt and lived in a camper perched on top an old pickup bed. Alongside her leaned fishing gear and she was walking the path of her life.

Sun dropped to an acute angle and created a blinding glare. Sun ball was low in the sky but still cast white, not a yellow or orange light, but a melting, burning posterization. Migla Fon and Lamon Fig were following a road along a canal that led to a beehive colony where small people lived when this light filled their eyes, and out of the light a woman appeared, walking towards them, who seemed to emerge from the sun. She wore a canvas hat, placed casually on her head, and in her hand carried a fishing pole. The late afternoon light solarized her form, shaping her edge into halo and she moved towards Lamon, blinding him. He thought she must be an apparition stepped off the sun's surface but it was Cotteeman, 400-year-old Cotteeman, approaching him here.

Cotteeman walked past royal palms planted by rich industrialists, palms planted to replace trees struck and killed by lightening so many years ago, in an ancient Seminole village. One hundred and sixty years ago, not so long ago, really, Seminole had had the place all to themselves, all these fishes, and oranges too. The wind stroked the palms and scratched and tickled the flapping fronds, and strolling through royal palms that grew out of a lawn she thought she could put a tent down here, yes, a little spot like this, it was people she wanted to avoid, after all, in order to paint. It was an exodus . . . a hibernation . . . no, an exodus: a lot of survivors were on the road every month of the year, on the highways and byways, heading towards the parklands following the scenic routes.

A swarm of swallows swooped down upon the trees and shrubs in the savannah, behaving like bees, feeding in a random, tangential chaos; unsynchronized acrobats, bereft of artistic expression, unlike a flock that murmured as one. The swallows fed on the fly, in small groups, then postured along a wire between two poles, and congregated to rest awhile and digest. These birds were prototype of the NSA and remained long after governments ceased to exist, and there were things they heard whether government wanted to hear them or not . . .

Turtles fed in a pond, lounging on its edge, turtles as big as any snapper Migla had ever seen. Kingfishers and teal ducks in the tall reeds watched as turtles with outstretched necks and splayed fingers and toes caught sunbeams, absorbed them and in prostate pose worshipped the Sun Life. Blue and orange needles darted about playfully, launching from green lily pads and landing on turtle's back.

The swallows swarmed and fed, moving like bees move. Over there a young cormorant was trying to balance on a high wire, weaving to and fro, its tail bobbing back and forth as it wove, its bill agape, but soon enough juvenile got its bearings and found its balance. Pileated woodpecker darted along the boardwalk where Cotteeman walked, creating playful, undulating waves of motion out in front of him as he strolled through palm trees and mahogany. Woodpecker liked to eat ants that lived in the aerial nests of orchid and bromeliad.

Blooming Flower, its dirty parts, seemed much nicer at night to Cotteeman, past the savage heat of sun. Silhouettes of palm brushed water-colored skies and, softening focus and widening aperture, foreground and background blurred their shapes and the lost detail created enchanting vistas and what man had done and what man had built was covered in wind, and cooled down for a while. Yes, this place was much nicer at night, man and women were savage and had made such a mess of things.

Deer watched the flamingo arrive from across the savannah while crows flew overhead. Deer ran out onto the savannah to greet flamingo, but quickly scattered for cover as a survivor crouching in the nearby mangrove stood up. Deer hadn't seen this one and watched from behind the brush as the survivor rose from where she hid and waved her arms wildly at turtle: *over here.* Then she disappeared and deer ran out over to flamingo, much faster now, across the road and up ahead in no time; this was their territory and flamingo was passing through on their way home. Crow flew here and loved it too. They flew in morning's soft rain after a hard night of heavy rain, a loud rain that struck lightning and shook the earth on this long pine key. Moving grass ran though it all and they had had the place to themselves for so long now that they felt safe. Where did those deer go? Tucked into brush somewhere?

It was another beautiful day. Some days Clipena was a Florida Bay tour guide, but today her white pelicans along with crocodiles were lounging lazily and sunbathing along a sandy bank of marlstone. Nearby, osprey tore at fish and ate its flesh, seagulls squawked and squealed overhead and manatee was body-surfing but everyone stopped what they were doing and followed Clipena and her pelicans towards the horizon when Migla and Lamon were spotted floating on a wavy line, coming towards them. Migla cried when she saw manatee and then cried again. She was an emotional bird and often cried. Chirping in the foreground, red-shouldered hawks, several of them, beautiful creatures, were breathing the same air Migla breathed and she and Lamon ran now, trotting fast across the bay, running for their lives, across borders, only to run into another bird hunter. But somehow they escaped . . . for a while anyway . . . and ran from this particular trap, ran to escape captivity, ran to get home.

How many today in America have had to run, really run, for their lives? How many, sitting on fat piles, fat seats of consumptive, phantom, electronic debt created from binary code, zero for you and one for me understood the duality: the serfs must pay for the excess created by the super rich. A lot of mock was abroad and foreigners bought the country out from under Americans and drove them and flamingo out and pushed Seminole deeper into the swamps only to hunt and kill them still. It broke her heart then, but gladdened her heart to return.

Migla liked the glades and big cypress area. The natural world, Pahayokee, stirred her and Lamon Fig more than anything else, and what men and women had done with agriculture, and the larger culture, how they had celebrated their lives, was in fact of grave consequence . . . it had impacted everything. All the development, all the building and spreading that crowded out the natural order of things and native beauty: birds, mahogany, palms, sawgrass, fish, manatees and bullheads had always seemed obscene to her but she understood why people had fallen in love with Blooming Flower, and America for that matter, but boy, oh boy, were the mutations ever gross. Government had really messed up and rather than create a country for all, one that treasured and protected its native beauty, it represented the corporatists and their global economy and the rich, screwing it up for ordinary people in a big way.

It was gone now, over, capitalism had failed, and although cloud cover protected Migla from the sun, a furiously fast cloud cover, running clouds that skipped on the wind, the air was still heavy. *Wow, have I never been here before? I must have been.*

But what will save the survivors?

Theocean was clever and knew enough to explain complex issues in terms survivors could better understand and they came to be well-informed about what had happened in America and caused her to decline.

He said, "For those of you who still don't know let me offer a critique. America is a country of citizens, not consumers. We are citizens, not a spread sheet. A country must put the needs of its own citizens first, always, and treasure them and the land and wild life too, lest it all be pillaged like it was."

"Mock reproduces the same way an invasive seed grows into weeds, and spreads, producing thousands of more seeds with every new plant and before you know it, it can't be got rid of. A wastrel nation that does not respect the value of its citizens, its wildlife, and its wilderness will be vanquished, and that civilization will fail, beginning with just one bad, out-of-control thing."

"The government modelled conspicuous consumption, taking it to a whole new level and, washing the world in mock and debt, the American people were egregiously loaned upon. Debt was an asset for government but for people a liability. Corporations didn't want to pay it and headquartered abroad. Maybe they were smarter than most: they did not want to be burdened with the government's debt and certainly didn't want their assets expropriated."

"Believe me when I say this, it was mock that destroyed America."

Chapter 22

Crila Wrog infiltrated the Miamia camps where serfs had organized themselves into gangs. There were other types there too, trapped in the southern, escape-the-North-American-winter refugee camps of Blooming Flower, when capitalism failed and gasoline disappeared, and from where it was not possible to get back home unless one walked, or flew. Crila was crow girl.

Like great heron, Crila rose in the morning and greeted the day. Heron stood at the edge of a pond, its wings bent at its elbows and, wrapping its wing tips in front, nodded and folded in prayer. Crila watched and thought it a reverential way to start the day, a day that will never come again, and adopted heron's reflective, prayerful pose. Near dawn light bugs flew towards her, lighting up the paths she walked upon before day broke, blinking faint, fading, residual flickers from yesterday's night. In the evening Crila prayed in the same way, like heron did, and the flies turned on their lights again, and signaled good evening.

Motorcycles rushed past her prayer site, their engines revving noisily, powerfully, rumbling fast over roads that ran through moving grass. Survivors stopped to stare when they rode by, always with their mouths agape. The constant fair weather brought out cyclists . . . in the north it was too cold to ride this time of year but this breed migrated and trailed the seasons round the continent, spring, summer, autumn then winter, a group emblematic of freedom, the open road, what America had stood for, for so many, in their minds, for so long now . . . and lost to most. But not these men and women, and Agod saw to it that they had access to gasoline.

A motorcycle ride was pleasant, thought Crila, getting up from her prayers, get up on a bike and ride. A few women rode by. *They were not broads*, Crila thought, *I would ever mess with,* she coughed, choking on a laugh. *I'd wanna be on their side,* and choked again. They captured her imagination and appealed to her sense of freedom, and independence. *I could work with these women and men . . . as they follow the seasons round the continent.* Crila was lying down and listening to the crickets, and thinking.

It was Tuesday.

Megacity Miamia had stalled, the drug mock from the southern Americas had ceased to flow to it. Miamia was addicted to it and its withdrawal a tough one: for a junkie, mock money bought drugs but for corporatists mock was the drug; oh, rich, privileged brats and camp slaves still rode motorcycles, crisscrossing Pahayokee and making a mess of things, mindless of those who worshipped and respected it but their hedonism required fuel so they hid reserves deep in the Pahayokee swamps.

Some trillions of mock had flowed into the United States from South America over the years and powerful bankers knew how to launder it; yes, they got their cut alright, from the expanded-mock-supply marked as debt to the taxpayers, and their stealth economy sunk the real one.

A catbird yanked at the flesh of an orange, tearing it, tilting its head, and quickly swallowing. This went on for several minutes . . . it stopped, gave pause then swallowed; it was a gorgeous creature: black hat, rusted rump, satiated pale breast and long tails, and sang a delightful song after its meal then flittered out from under a bush over to a dripping water spout and took a drink. Crila got up and got on her bike.

She moved among these people, they were part of her cover. Crow girl had infiltrated the social circles of both the elite in Miamia and the refugee camp serfs just outside its borders; she got around. A wild woman, her boyfriend ate mushrooms, and she drank the water he passed for the visions it induced: she needed the mushroom's power in order to smell Stoonman, because wherever Stoonman or Papel were, Tossherrheim was never far behind. She rode with Latina girls by day and in great style. They ate caterpillars and swallowed them whole; caterpillar crawled around inside and tickled them – and they were always laughing. Crila and her friends loved to laugh, and her wildness metamorphosed into extraordinary glamour when she moved in the same circles as the rich, the elites, and celebrities.

Twenty miles away the few Key West deer that had managed to survive were still locked up, but forgotten, as was Florida panther. Not far away a king and queen of a south Florida refugee camp lived in a recreational vehicle: a mean-looking pair, from somewhere up north – and they were Crila's neighbors for a week.

Wildlife refuges had been squeezed in amongst slick roadways overflowing with speeding autos, carrying over-consuming people, rushing towards fast food and amusement, squishing turtle and snake, shattering panther and deer and, although cars had been banned from the roads for years now, no one had had the sense to set them free. At the North Pole summit Agod had told Pilson Bloo to do just that, get down there and release them, and she did. She unlocked the gates and deer and panther cried out for joy and joined the Wilderness League, with revenge on their minds. Even wild pig enlisted. They had been shot at for so many years now, just for the sport of it, and wanted to get even.

Day in and day out the king kept his queen high up upon her toilet throne. For so long now, the couple was influenced and informed by a warped sense of entitlement channeled through an aberrant strain of collective consciousness. Oh, she was beautiful alright, but beauty was easy when one was young, when youth shone through transcendiary time, only to falter later, and never come again. But what was inside? In a time of dwindling resources, excess and entitlement had become unpopular, and fast, and the queen upon her toilet throne had to do better than that.

This king and queen, Cril said to her friends, *I mean, they're something else. Look, they don't use the communal commode, they have their own poop pot in their recreational vehicle and every few days they rinse their tanks out in the center of the campground for all of us to whiff and sniff . . . their poop. Who do they think they are?*

Riding in back through a wealthy area along a street perpendicular to one that ran off a boulevard shaded by banyon and *oh my Agod, they are beautiful,* Crila thought, the mature vegetation and plantings growing in the area impressing her. On a parallel avenue people strolled towards the south and, where it intersected with another road, spoke in many languages: Spanish, Italian, English, German, French, Russian, and all the other languages of the world.

She could hear the sun and was very happy the cold north and its snow were so far away.

She wasn't sloppy but a good hunter; she not only stalked, but changed shape and, using traps, lured her prey. No one followed her. It was impossible unless she wanted it that way.

She blended in and slipped around but didn't speak much or engage; she was often detached and invisible especially around the rich but when the time was right could cast a spell, manufacturing allure and glamour. Some thought her unfriendly, but she was just doing her job.

Crila got off her bike and disappeared into the crowd, into the show of wealth, making obtuse cuts through its pathways. She observed from the perimeter, lurking on the shadowy side of the street, along the edge of the crowd then by way of osmosis floated across on an arc to a spiritual plane, a plane of spirits, an algorithm of perpendicular and parallel lines and acute angles where everything converged.

She laughed. A young guitarist, who wasn't very good, sang and played near a fountain. Its constant surge, tumbling and falling, tumbling and falling, the sun, and the young man's stylized Mexican tune sung in English caught her attention but his poor performance caused her mind to shift and wander to other places. Motorcycles roared, horns beeped, bells rang, birds chirped, and voices chatted and murmured intimately while the player continued to strum his guitar and sing off-pitch. Rich-thin South Florida brats, sleek and attractive, well-fed, sustained and nurtured in a place of good food, strolled obliquely by, gazing in at window displays.

No one knew the other and everyone had more than their fair share and rich kept to themselves so as not to have to explain how they came by their largess . . . which kind of thievery. People left one another alone; they feared being discovered or found out.

The mushrooms gave her the power to see and not be seen. This was important and although she was, at first, uncomfortable once she adjusted to the plant's power, she relaxed. She needed to blend in, and get an impression of the place, but was gorgeous and needed a disguise for this first look, so changed her shape and flew overhead to see the detail otherwise unseen. And there he was, Tossherrheim.

It was Wednesday. She had blended in, but tomorrow would make a splash.

The next day she strolled in and what an entrance. She was glamourous and cast a spell. People stopped and stared like they did when hundreds of motorcycles roared by in parade . . . enchanted. Looked, but didn't touch, didn't approach, they had forgotten how, technology had dullened all their senses. Yes, their senses had atrophied, but they were still rich.

It was dangerous to be beautiful. She knew this. Lousy singer was still singing near the fountain with lots of accompanying street noise. People chatted, and with the warm air tossing on the wind, she felt the sun and was having fun on this boulevard of excess. She let off her scent and was soon followed, followed and approached by a thin Miamia rat.

They talked and talked. He said he was more than 50 years old, but had never been outside Blooming Flower and had never seen snow. They talked about different ethnic groups in America and how some assimilated and some didn't. Then thin Miamia rat pointed to a dark computer screen. No more technology, he sighed. No more surveillance, she thought happily. She was paying attention. She needed to seduce this thin Miamia rat and everyone else in this place and turn them against Papel, Stoonman, and Tossherrheim, and convince them to live Another Way, the parkland way in this paradise of excess. Her job was a big one but Crila's crew would be here soon to help.

The cars were expensive, but not running on the road. *Real easy to pick up men and women here, a great place for seduction; effortless, their senses have atrophied, they can't think for themselves, too much TV. My friends will come here, with their friends, and in no time we will infiltrate this place, take it over, and run this longitudinal and latitudinal coordinate for Geela.* Crila was having a marvelous time, strolling through the streets where the last of the beautiful people lurked on the arm of a thin Miamia rat. She walked a parallel path past the fourth richest estate in south

Florida, no longer occupied, and then followed a perpendicular line, towards a fifth, larger estate running obliquely towards the sea.

"Where you going?" asked the thin Miamia rat, sounding like someone she knew.

Did you know panthers run for several seconds before their brains overheat and they pass out? Crila ran towards the ocean, jumped in and dove through the surf and under the water looked around then broke the surface and came up for air. There was so much salt and so much sun, so much sting in her eyes that she couldn't see what was in front of her, but she could see under the water. Her eyes stuck closed, so much salt and so much sun it stung her eyes and she dove again and under the surf powerful hallucinations like ammonia swirled around in her brain, strong and vibrant.

She dragged her body from the surf and lay down on the beach, Crila and everyone else on the beach, on towels or beach blankets, above them only sky, way above the sky, but in between sky and people lying on blankets was space where all the voices, all the chatter on the beach, lingered, compressed by the boom of the waves into a space just above blankets but beneath the sky, the din another plane between sky, a bouclé spun sky, and sand below.

She looked up at the bouclé looped and curled layer of buckled and fuzzy weave. When she was very young, in her early teens, she was on a beach and never forgot the first time she heard this din, lying on the sand and, having no other memory of ever feeling as relaxed as she did then, after a recent swim, in her youth, had paid attention. She was calling it a bouclé sky; the white, and the yellow-white, yellow light, real, real, pale yellow, some of the yellow, in the diffused part of the light, white; in the gray cloud or the white part of the gray, all of it, so much of it fuzzy, as if out of focus, but in fact just bouclé.

Over and away from where the sun was making all these colors, through the gray, the white and the pale yellow clouds, over on the other side she saw baby blue, baby blue peeking through and back from where the sun streamed its rays through fuzzy diffusion, bouclé, out of focus bouclé, but, over there in the baby blue, she heard the voices, and the one voice with the message.

She took off the wet shirtdress she swam in, and the underwear and bra, and pulled on a dry denim dress, the black one she liked so much, leaving nothing on underneath.

Thin Miamia rat dragged her off the beach after her impulsive swim and together, for a little longer they listened to the lousy street singer.

Crila was straight from the sea but hadn't rinsed off, only her feet. Another woman, in line for the water spout, in front of her, was moving in a relaxed manner and

82

finished her shower slowly, only to move a few inches from the water spout then bend to dry her feet, pull on her socks and tie her sneakers one at a time. She was old and, oh, so slow, so Crila didn't turn on the shower head just the spigot closer to the ground, so not to splash the old woman. She was not impatient but the line for the spout was growing behind her, actually looping around the beach head. Crila gave up and left the sticky saltwater film on her skin.

Thin Miamia rat had never met a woman like her before.

It was the swimming and diving she had missed. It had been so cool and she was in places where she couldn't swim because of sharks and crocodiles, but mostly it was too cool and had forced a narrower experience because swimming pulled her to Blooming Flower, and under. If the crocodiles and the sharks were around, or it was cold, she had a narrower experience, but she was glad to have reintroduced it today. It refreshed her, she loved it as ritual. When she was wriggling, and at the same time trying to conceal herself from passersby, out of her wet swimming clothes into a dry dress, did she notice she could really move a lot better than last year. Last year she was stiff, she was hurting, she knew it was the size of the tent she was sleeping in and the fact that she hadn't been seducing for about a year and, *Oh my Agod, that was a stupid thing to do,* and traveling in that cramped little coupé was a bad idea too.

She wouldn't take off her hat or sunglasses – she had just been in the ocean and felt unkempt. Her feet hurt from all the walking; she had blisters on her heels and toes and needed small strips, so back to the bike where she kept small strips. She grabbed her purse, breathed in and breathed out and, slowing down, watched the sky for her crew. She was afraid it wouldn't be possible to convince these people to live Another Way but in fact she could. It was just an emotional, psychological doubt that swept her momentarily. She had great power, from Agod and from the plants and there was no way the world couldn't change if people wanted it, she was sure of this, and the survivors were too.

One must have a lot of dough to keep a place in south Florida and the only way Crila could get close to this place was by staying at an escape-the-north-american-winter refugee camp in Blooming Flower. People here were from all over the world and wealthy, and the vendors sophisticated, merchant class sophisticates who weren't offering made-in-china merchandise to their customer base, she observed.

It was Thursday.

She liked the way mushrooms and a little pot made her feel, and she kept it up. She needed plant's wisdom to get this task done. Horns beeped from cars that were parked, permanently parked. Street sounds abound and she slept in the camps by night and roamed the rich streets by day. All the crows in her tribe would be here soon and seduce these people, changing their world and, using trickery, inform them – a whole population reseeded with right-thinking thoughts.

Early scouts had begun to arrive and miles upon miles of crows were following them, approaching from all the directions, thin, spidery, sky-crawling black lines, lines whose bodies fattened and grew as the procession streamed closer and became one, whole, dense, wide, black iridescent smudge darkening the sky over the rich make-believe area, where all the streams converged at a single spot in Blooming Flower.

The crows flew in long stretches of miles and miles of crows, from all over the continent. It was their time.

Crila disappeared from the rich avenue and left the world of dullened senses and quickly hopped up on the Tampa-Miami Trail and left the make-believe world behind, taking thin Miamia rat. She sighed. Blooming Flower reminded her of another place and time, in California, a lot of rich there too, where winter was warm.

Make-believe dissolved. She had thin Miamia rat with her and took him into her world. Motorcycles roared and *the world will die if it doesn't change. Hope my crows can transform a make-believe world into a real one and Geela's anxiety for the future dissolves . . . but I am still a long way from tomorrow.*

Back at the camp an old man was talking about food. He said there was free food right there, and pointed past the parkland and said the name of the place several times, all the time pointing. Crila asked him to repeat it . . . she hadn't understood . . . and after several repetitions, still didn't hear it right.

Thank you, Agod, for plant power and intelligence, for marijuana, for the swim in the sea, for Blooming Flower, for the impulse and the power behind the impulse that triggered the day that brought me here; for the senses that haven't atrophied, for the herbs, and for you. And thank you for the survivors, the others, whose senses have not atrophied. I need them.

The parkland was close to the urban parts of Blooming Flower, close enough to view the culture and oversee her mission but in another direction was an area of big cypress and solitude, isolated and alone, a paradise from where she got her inspiration and power. A place like that had a lot to offer a crow girl like her. It was a crow girl's spirit, the way she felt inside, how alive she was that attracted people. She knew a few things about fashion and glamour and understood the powers of enchantment and seduction. She felt grand, couldn't get over it really, how good she felt; she had been feeling down but now was sure she could accomplish her mission. Something happened over there between the swimming and stroll around the make-believe world that made her feel alive again, and hopeful.

Crila made an effigy when she was sure the words on the papers she held in her hands were completely encoded in her DNA, sure its knowledge and wisdom would never fade, and she lit a fire: it was ritual and fun for her. It was the first time she had built a fire since she left the north. She had been camping for thirty days and noticed most campers built fires for comfort and were pulled into trance by their flames. It was a social thing, a collective trance, but for Agod's sake she burnt wood to keep her hearth warm in the north and took a break from that chore here.

She collected palm fronds from the nearby area and, for Agod's sake, had no idea they were so flammable. What was in her hands meant something to her; her past, my Agod, the stuff she burnt, she first wrote down in 1984, think of that, all those years ago. *It's about time I got to work on this stuff.* In the background music played, voices sang, people chatted over dinner, and quiet conversations floated above the campfires.

Agod had been patient with her. Subtext she normally shared within the context of a more familiar relationship, words shared with strangers, were sometimes misunderstood, but not always. To a couple of guys at the parkland, cousins, friendly, and drinking a lot . . . she didn't care but, yes, they were drinking a lot . . . Crila mentioned Immokalee and with one voice the cousins said it was a scary place.

But they are migrant workers, field hands who pick the food you eat. Why are you afraid? Is it the people or the place? The people who pick the food you eat, and all those rich people out there, she swept her wings over Blooming Flower, *who didn't think about the consequences of their actions and took the land for granted and built ridiculously expensive homes on ridiculously large lots, to live in part-time and apart because, well, just because they could, separated, and in a big way. Immokalee pickers grow and gather food for those in houses empty now, because rich is almost gone. They huddle together in expensive enclaves and hang on to what they can and the pickers . . . the pickers are eating well.*

It will be easy to reseed this place, Crila thought and looked over at thin Miamia rat, then back again at the two cousins. *What am I gonna do with them?* In the past, often, what she had thrown away had been more valuable than what she kept . . . and she didn't want to make that mistake again.

It was Friday.

Downtown was sunny and warm and the crows found the place by the smell of cigar smoke . . . swirling, twirling upwards . . . and signs of the rich and wealthy abounded, signaling Tossherrheim was nearby.

Crow came in a big, black iridescent smear, and like cloud, darkened the sky, rubbing out the light. Everywhere people ran and shrieked and hid. In great numbers crow spread out over the land, and got it right too. Grabbing people, they hung them upside down, wrapped their talons around their feet and thrusting back and forth, copulated and introduced new seed.

Neighborhoods were scoured, and the weak ripped from their homes. Crow dropped the weaklings from sky to ground, killing their seed. Necks snapped and flipped, cracking bones. Some crows did it like a duck and snatching women shoved their heads underwater in the ponds and nearby sea and, mounting, introduced new seed. Sticky foam stuck to sticky watery film, lung sacks puffed, asphyxiated, and while pleasure increased and clung in snarly balls, orgy panted and held its breath; rapture emerged and spewed towards the sky.

Rich leaped like frogs and jumped into the air, and eager, ready for a fantastic orgasm, bobbed up and down, over and over and mated with crow, while others stood by and simply watched. Crow cornered some and pinned them down and, surrendering to change, they accepted new seed. Nonproductive females were cast out and crushed – survival of the fittest.

The girls grabbed the boys by their necks and tossed them to the ground and mounting, showed them what to do, knowing some just wanted to get off but had no idea how to do it, really do it.

The music was pink now, pink laughter and pink chatter, loud pink noise that rose over the breeding frenzy, loud like punk rock: *kill the pink birds . . . pink feathers for pink hats . . . oh, baby, yuh . . .*

Crow grabbed the fertile pods and brushed them with wings, depositing new seed, a tangle of wings and screeches wrestling and forcing the rich to submit, smearing and grabbing and thrusting and coming and going all afternoon, humping and bumping, *boom boom boom,* appendages thrusted completed orgasms of the tired and rich and, kicking off the spent, made room for more punching, fighting, biting, kicking, twirling, swirling orgasms and, rubbing genitals, released new seed. Males hunted females and the women hunted the men, men and women who had slept for eons, and woke.

Crow was repository and carried the seed of North American super humans, the gods and power animals, all those who had been obliterated by a culture that had supplanted them, to fertilize the chosen and save the country and create new super humans to lead survivors to the parklands and Another Way.

The boys gave chase and hounded the girls, unrelentingly so, and forcing themselves upon them, introduced new seed. In a great hall the remaining rich and remaining crows lined opposite walls and one by one chose with whom one or the other would mate. These were the lucky ones, the ones the super humans and gods in North America had chosen to lead.

Crows carried eggs and sperm from the long gone super humans and North American gods who had risen from their graves. Yes, the gods woke up. They were sick and tired of weaklings and sniveling whiners, this was no way to build a country: fostering and encouraging people who complained, and judged, and when they had nothing in the world to complain about, to complain even more, and by way of crow gave their seed to those grateful and thankful few survivors, introducing a new beginning. And the crows, heavy with new seed, made the journey. Some unknown instinct drove them here and the calls of the rich lured them in, burping and farting sweet smells, from good foods.

These rich had obliterated the culture it supplanted with enthusiasm and zeal. They created secret banks, secret governments, a stealth economy, and stole its wealth; they expanded mock and spread its debt all over the world, pooping all over everyone. Oh, a few ball clubs were named after the deceased and a few monuments erected, but not until the super humans and North American gods were all dead and gone, safely in the ground: Heron Lake, Flamingo Park, Eagle Mountain, Red Braves and of course all the rubber-wheeled ponies.

Spent, a tribe emerged, carrying seed from long gone North American super humans and gods.

It was Saturday.

Two miles ahead on an eleven mile road, Crila headed east past a mid-way campground. *Please Agod, let my tent shelter keep the bugs out,* she thought to herself. It was hard last year camping without a tent shelter, sleeping out in the open. *The bugs,* she sucked in her breath and a little saliva pulled past her teeth, *were unpleasant.*

A blue crab restaurant was on the left and thousands of bikers had stopped to eat. Crila stopped, too, for blue crab, stone crab, pink shrimp, and grouper . . . yum . . . amber jack, alligator tail, and frog legs . . . oysters too. Cicada buzzed a heat tossed wind in animated sun while a collaboration of renegade and law abiding bikers, devoted to the open road, icons of sacred life and sacred experience, emblematic, stylized American freedom, stood on display, and conversed, and reminded all who Americans really were, and what they could do if they put their minds to it and worked together.

They looked good and representing sacred freedom, drove the icon, rode the icon, and kept it alive. Woman was devotional, as was man, a cultural, sensual, symbol of sexuality and aroused fecundity on the back of a bike and, summoned, they delivered Crila's gang of crows.

No mosquitoes, but midgets got in when the tent flap was open. *It won't be good if they can get in through the mesh,* she thought. Crila was in Flamingo, pink Flamingo, and cried . . . it was so beautiful. She thought she had died and gone to heaven despite the headache she had all day and, up until now, still couldn't speak.

She tried to retrieve a thought. Motorcycles had driven by last night, in large numbers, their vapors invading her nostrils and ears and through those orifices invading her brain, settling in a couple of areas and depositing pain and the kind of pain that set up before throb arrived but didn't bloom . . . it was borderline. She was able to get up and run but it was uncomfortable.

This place was more hospitable in the evening, at night, after the sun went down. So many couldn't tolerate paradise in July, August or September, or even June, but Crila liked it: too hot for most, or too ugly, when night was cool and neighborhoods more attractive. Like snow, darkness covered, cloaked the debris, the mess people had made, but paradise was not a vicarious, abstract notion, a room with a view. It was all around and she in the middle. Crila's wasn't a tidy well-cropped frame through a filtered lens, but one where all darkness and light pulsed through her conscious and subconscious minds.

Before capitalism failed she had felt stuck but, in a post-capitalist America, well, it could certainly grind a girl down if one was camping with people who were not survivors, who will not survive. They were here, of course, the ones who had figured it out but there were people here too who had no clue. Camping and other outdoor experiences allowed for a slower pace. People shared ideas and slowed down long enough to consider alternative points of view, amongst Agod's nature, not man's made world. Oh, some had hiked it and climbed it furiously, seeking that extreme experience, but didn't always see. Well, they got their extreme experience now. Still, Crila imagined she could convince some of them to live Another Way, the parkland way, if she took the time to influence them.

Oh, if only the wind would pick up, Crila thought. She heard, and felt again, a surge, a light puff, more encouraging than the last one; the last whisper soft and low and barely audible, this one louder – the trees heard it and responded; tree did not bend but picked it up and let it rustle leaves, but trunk did not bow, not that kind of wind. The bugs in the night, thousands of them buzzed just outside the mesh, insane sound. She let it in and it took her places.

Keep them wild, keep the animals wild, if not, these varmints, squirrels and raccoons and skunks are gonna climb into this tent with me. They are not as timid as an armadillo – they got bigger brains, maybe? Crila breathed in deeply through her nose processing this thought: *I am sleeping in armadillo territory – armadillo and raccoons in the same territory,* and she laughed out loud.

Bikers snared a motorist who had run into a panther, and dragged him all through the towns and counties of South Florida—past the park where Crila stayed—alive for a while, then bikers were dragging a corpse. People cheered along the route, the survivors did anyway, the ones who pursued Another Way. Crila's crows had reseeded. There was a world of difference between those who could think for themselves and those who couldn't and were brainwashed by media.

Life flopped in the pond, a splashing and squeaking cacophony. Anhinga jostled with a frog, and whipping and nodding, snapping and turning, aligned itself and swallowed. On a dead limb over water's edge, another one preened and cleaned, while drakes and youngsters chatted and clattered, upside down, topsy-turvy baby talk, heads in the mud.

Anhinga draped aloft, over green teals, majestic anhinga in a capelet as fine as a king's coronation robe with a collar of fur. An entire kingdom of family and flock lived on the pond with plenty of adult supervision and scolded constantly. This was Eden, the paradise where it all got set up, America's Garden of Eden. Yes, Blooming Flower was America's Garden of Eden, a gift from Africa.

A flock of evening grosbeaks was in the sweet grass and one blackbird with white tail feathers flew past and skipped in and out of the bushes nearby while a cat skulked through tall grass, pouncing on mice and young rats. Throughout the morning Crila wandered over this paradise looking over things and the blackbird with white tail feathers flew across her path.

Bromeliads grew in the live oaks, beautiful nests of little orchids and pointy leaves. Squirrels scurried from one branch to the next, one frond to the next, perambulating, getting around like monkeys did. *Oh my Agod, they are under my feet now,* she whispered so her neighbors wouldn't hear and, thinking out loud, she knew she had to stop Stoonman and Papel from following her and getting to Geela. The white bears from the north would make their way south, and change shape soon. How can she help? She must change, what can she do? From where will she get the strength? Why Agod, of course.

Crila struggled and sought help from others. People have to change or else. Geela had wanted her to infiltrate south Florida. How successful was she?

89

It was Sunday and she slept all day.

Geela was eagle, Agod's daughter. Agod was both mother and father. Early North American super humans had worn eagle headdresses and earned one feather at a time for feats of bravery and valor and unselfish acts of kindness and goodness; the country's invaders certainly hadn't had a custom like that . . .

Crila changed shape and headed north.

A man walked along a high way's edge, carrying a backpack. His dog trotted after him, sniffing the ground, wagging its tail. He walked, and slept outdoors. Northward bound, they walked past patches of flower and color, randomly planted and scattered in pastures and lawns, seed strewn by wind, water and wildness, away from heat and a warm winter. A river ran through it, towards the marsh and spilled into ocean. The water was warm enough for a swim and he spent a night on its banks. Painted buntings nested nearby.

In the morning he stood at the confluence of St. Mary's and the Atlantic and crossed the bridge that spanned the waterway – it bisected an expansive marshland. This stretch was a pretty walk, a very pretty road close to the ocean, the coastline, the marsh and river, but it would get very ugly, very fast. He was already tired from walking and a bit surprised because, holy mackerel, he had a long, long way to go, a long walk ahead. The road he was on ran with train tracks and a freight line strung with hopper cars chugged past and tooted and blew its horn and, holy mackerel, it was carrying polar bears and heading south.

Something was going on over there on the St. Mary but he knew not what. It was some kind of depot, piled high with raw materials. The wind blew and motorcycles roared by at high speed, and the train blew its whistle. What was going on over there?

On the road deciduous trees had set their buds and spring began to tease. Bloom was on view here and leaves about to pop, buds set to open, ready to reveal color: lime green, nut brown, peach red, yellow skin of willow, yellow brown from maple, red from maple, brownish-yellow from oak. Color spilled and spring approached. Hawk hunted frogs along pond's edge, hawk who normally didn't like to get its feathers wet, but had hungry young to feed.

Nice season, April. He imagined bugs in May swarming the place and plenty of good hunting for fly catchers, and bats. Their colors—pink red, pale yellow and green, paused in textures varied from wispy to coarse, coarser still, then stiff—began as brown then muted to white brown buds before leaves unfurled then white brown synthesized to green brown, and leafy tree rocked. It was a tall tree and holy mackerel, it was beautiful. *Like sorbet*, he thought, and something else he couldn't recall, a muted-colored something else.

The colors were not the deep, dark, rich dead tones that appeared when the earth tilted and fall happened, displaying their finale, preluding sleeping cold, and death – fireworks of bursting dead dying, fizzling then fading before cold winter, but birthing, muted, white light awakening; inceptive light trapped and commanded tree absorb red and blue and reflect green and liminal light and, at a liminal spot on the informed spectrum of the visible and invisible, touched, and vibrating waves absolved dark night, and appeared.

Well, I see red and blue and green too, backpacker thought. Some could see it. Subdued spring colors emerged, and rain tapped the ground, scratching color. Nakedness, and naked boughs, naked limbs in amongst evergreen, ever-green evergreens . . . out of nakedness emerged ever-color green. Color came slowly, peeping slowly, creeping slowly through the veins in the branches . . . revealing . . . and it was a lot like magic.

Wild flowers were in bloom, yarrow, wild mustard, yellow something growing all over. The man with the backpack inspired and yellow something, clinging like tresses to trees, crawled and creeping like snakes along wastelands bordering the highway, gripped abandoned houses. He walked over and smelled it, a subtlety perfumed scent, and something else happened, he saw and heard scent that followed inspiration then halted. This flower's scent birthed on inspiration, then disappeared. Nothing. Ephemeral? *Am I ephemeral?*

Not many smelled it. It did not linger or tarry, did not loiter or prolong, didn't draw but receded, indiscernible to most, a phantom vapor with no discernable trail, did not persist or abide, but evanesced and faded. Melting, the man with the backpack got down on all fours and picked up its scent and prayed; but fleeting, it did not endure nor cling only glanced.

Crila Wrog perched low on a limb off a shallow rise in the northeastern part of the warm country. Nearby another crow, squeaking and chattering, and hanging upside down, called and cawed out, its tail feathers skyward, spinning round and round, cranking like a noisy party maker.

Blurred streaks of gray stripe blinked blue and green, leaving water stains on a predawn highway, and after a while the streaks were white and purple, not blue and green. The rain drove upon her feathers, tapping and drilling. Light streaked green and blue again then white was gone and oily black asphalt and predawn rain bent a lamp-lit red. Lamp light rained and a highway strip of oily ribbon reflected all like a river bed; green and red flashed and blinked and, faced-down, Crila looked into a river of tungsten and halogen, fluorescent stripes of asphalt ribbon streaks, and bikes screeched and hurtled by on wet, slippery tracks.

This was a dangerous ride in the rain and early dark light. Bikes passed on both sides and Crila couldn't see detail. She was frightened. Misty, moisty steam sprayed and rain kicked, drilling her eyeballs.

Oily roads meandered like ribbons through the nation's hub reflecting tungsten headlamps and taillights. Oil slicked and it was all a blur. Ahead and beyond they pressed on, signaling or not, left or right. Crila was outside the nation's capital and it was no sight-seeing excursion this morning, it was a try-and-stay-alive drive on this freeway. Actually, it was exciting to be out this time of day in the nation's capital, in the traffic, in the rush, watching the frenzy to market, raw materials, produce, finished goods, commuters, public servants and business people too. *And me. I like this, it stimulates me. Don't stay in your lane.*

It was Monday.

She left the limb and flew closer to the road, waiting for more bikes to ride by. On the lee side the heavy flow was headed south, but Crila northward bound. Her father, Vrucos, had often talked about interstates and what marvelous roads they were, great roads, fantastic roads to travel on and get around. Of course he had lived in another time, without freeways, and had traveled along winding, narrow roads interrupted by signal lights and stop signs for so long that in his mind interstates were the balls.

She flew over a pass. Its elaborate lanterns narrowed her focus: lit up and lined-up and evenly spaced. It was hard raining and the necks of the lamps were crooked, their light shining downwards, catching driving rain. For a minute it was easy to think she was looking at something other than what she saw . . . fountains maybe?

It was still raining when the sunball rose from behind black clouds and though it was more illuminated behind dark clouds it remained a stressful flight. Rain stroked, playing the road like a tightly strung instrument, making music of water, and wind, and the squealing vibratos humming below. Ahead the bikers took refuge and lined up under an overpass. It was a slippery, predawn rainfall, on a slippery interstate, and was smart to get off but there was not enough room under the pass to hold all the bikes – some wanted in but were forced back out on the road, into the rain, to seek shelter.

Cril Wrog hopped down, chose a bike, jumped on and her shape changed into a beautiful woman's. Light wasn't black anymore, but gray . . . it had turned the color of lead. It was still raining. She liked the water music and as they drove and rode along the oily, slicked greasy road, she liked the road a lot too. There was much going on in the nation's capital and along its eastern seaboard: many, many layers of a lot.

A sweep of rain created a crescent and colored light blurred its way through to another universe. An enormous flock of birds appeared overhead from the east, not starlings she was sure, or redwings, no, they were her crows, all her relatives, over the tree tops. They did not flap but glided while the big circular flock moved over the highway. The bike she was on steered its way around two salt distributing depots and then she found herself on a white bridge with white lines painted on white cement under a white surface. White snow and white sky and seagulls flocked about and a big black river flowed under her, and under the bridge. She could no longer see trees or tree line, no green.

And the freight train filled with polar bears followed the graceful curve in the crook of the lamp's neck and, roaming over the road, were guided by a gorgeous, ornate light.

Chapter 23

Winter circled the sky and late season crops. Its great bright stars, Pleiades and Orion, Sirius, Gemini and Polaris were larger than life and it seemed to Ligatus Latin larger than the Wilderness League and more beautiful too, if that was possible, maybe too beautiful, really, incredibly so.

Ligatus lay on his back, somewhere in paradise, and considered a tribe of very little people, Bee People, not so small actually but magic people who could shrink and make themselves fit on a bee's back. His bats had been talking about them for weeks now and Ligatus was keen to meet them.

They ate honey and lived in Greylock, an old growth spruce forest, in colonies and hives, and thrived. They flew with the bees and had stories that told about flying and being pelted by rain, hail and neonicotinoids, insecticides, herbicides, taxes, and everything else the system threw at them and still, for Agod's sake, somehow managed to survive. The small people rode on bees' backs, and when bats had introduced the smaller people to Ligatus they told him all, and everything they saw. Beehive Tribes, and other agricultural tribes, were holding the whole fragile cycle of life together . . . and without any help from failed corporatists.

The small people set out a water bowl in the forest for the bees and sometimes blue birds bathed in it and, standing on its rolled rim, drank from it too. Gold-finched winter feathers flocked and clasped, clinging to nodding stalks of bobbing seed heads and, flitting here and there, winter's white illuminated and washed their color clean.

Ligatus Latin flew on a pony at night, in his dreamtime, and traveled fast in daylight. Like the wild turkeys behind Agod's tent who, when preparing for take-off, trotted a bit, rocking sideways a little, wiggly, wobbly, running and running and running, clumsily lifting towards tree tops to roost, Ligatus and his pony, the one who sang, got a running start when they headed for the skies, sometimes through a tangle of wires and poles and, barely avoiding a crash, were off and flew fast, singing their favorite songs while the landscape beneath them careened and blurred.

On this night a woman in white was driving a white pickup, in daylight. The woman wore a cap and steering her truck on the wrong side of the road and traveling in the wrong direction, paid no mind at all to those shouting expletives and Ligatus wondered if he would end up like her and live long enough to drive on the wrong side of the road.

The clouds moved at furious speed and Ligatus couldn't see as clearly as he'd like, but he could see the rose bushes riding in the back of the truck the old lady drove on the wrong side of the road – they moved the sun. The small fragile buds on compact bush withstood the wind, and on the ride of their lives, a bedful of rose on the wrong side of the road gladdened his heart and he sang even louder, he sang to those roses, past bud and in bloom, riding in the back on the wrong side of the road; like livestock in a cattle car, their life force shimmered and stirred, trembling in supplanted light and transplanted wind.

Near a springhead, moving eastward on an old cattle path, long hopper beds chock full of orange headed for market, passing empty trucks returning to groves. Where Ligatus didn't see orange groves he saw grassland and fat cattle grazing on highland and hammock, miles and miles of fat, grass-fed cattle, long-horned and no-horned, every color and all breeds, on chaparral, on scrub and savannah. The land was flat and rich, and a breadbasket that fed those who couldn't grow their own food.

Two miniature deer wound their way towards the park land at dusk. It was a new year's eve and horned owl sat on a limb not far from where he camped, sat on a dead limb in scrub pine while Ligatus' pony grazed under the tree. The wind blew out of the southwest and stirred, shaping owl's feathers, but owl did not move, only feathers. Hundreds of bats flew in the sky, every whichy way, Ligatus' bats, and something two or three times larger than a bat, with a bill, a wood-cocked timber doodle.

A large, extended family made camp nearby and, with a squeaky dog that squealed as much as the kids did, played soccer in a Spanish-speaking dark, late into the night.

Ligatus was surrounded by many happy people and much beauty on this New Year's Eve, and when he fell asleep he opened his arms wide like the sky, dropped his reins and flew on his pony all over the land.

This night certainly won't come again, he thought and raced over poles and wires and, buzzing houses and cliffs, soaked up the same sun that illuminated the woman in the cap and the roses in the back of the truck and the crops in the fields and the revelers playing soccer in the Spanish-speaking dark.

Ligatus was a member of the League, and a spy. His bats picked up signals his mind could not sense. Using sound waves and feelers they guided with intelligence he didn't see but their good friend was reckless and while dreaming wouldn't listen – he was having way too much fun while he flew on his pony, all over the land.

Still his bats screeched, and called out. He flew low beneath wires, risked tangles, made it through – back on top, he was free. Through take-off and flight and all his close calls, he raced skyward, stretched his arms, off-lifted and flew.

A small flock of goldfinch wearing winter feathers flew by and turning looked at Ligatus on his wings, on his arms, on his own in the sky; finch, having left Greylock, were on their way too and glad to see others with them way up high in the sky.

Evening broke and night followed and when morning arrived, Ligatus dismounted and stood firmly on the ground. *Last night something had been trying to communicate with me without words,* he remembered. *Its spirit evoked . . . evoked what Ligatus? Someone, or something, will help me see past the limitations of my intelligence. Who was this,* he thought, *the bees or bats perhaps?*

Ligatus sought intelligence, and information. He was an agent for change and his motto was live the parkland way, Another Way, or else. Ants were marching towards California to aid the agricultural tribes and water the orchards that grew nuts and fruits and dates, and bees were on their way there too. He brokered the sale of fruits from orchards belonging to others and vegetables the pickers grew. It was his cover. He was a lot like Crila Wrog but operated independently, promoting the same cause. He too moved between two worlds and singing in code with help from his bats carried messages to those living Another Way.

No longer did technology control people, so many had abandoned it. The world had survived millennia without it, and had managed quite well. Finally, no tracking devices or surveillance and those who could think for themselves thrived, using the best kind of intelligence, innate intelligence. He had abandoned technology years ago, because in the end, it had aided globalists and abetted oppression, allowing them to put most on a road to serfdom . . . speeding the earth towards a quicker demise. Ligatus was walking the path of his life and, slowing down a while, waited for the others to catch up. Partnering with the bats had complemented his efforts and complemented him, too.

Mist fell on the highland hammock morning, mist with no fog. He lost his sight nonetheless but could still hear through the cloud-covered, diffused light. There was little heat, and the revelers, the Spanish-chatting family next door, watched over their children as they played at hunting with bows and arrows. A teen-aged son led the chase and a grandfather without a spouse advised. A happy group, laughing, talking and playing, watchful parents interacted with their playful family late into evening, stimulating them intellectually, but did not interfere. They simply watched over the play, the way it should be, Ligatus thought, unsupervised.

People, with if not the means to travel but a strong urge to survive, headed for the parklands to live Another Way: it was imperative. The whole surviving population on the continent was here in the parklands, all here, throngs and masses of survivors everywhere. Hungry people went where the food was and were fed well, while others looked on the parklands as museums, historic sites, where surviving Americans had finally arrived.

Appreciative Americans were here too and with wonder, awe, and amazement possessed great reverence for what this country, its land, and wilderness had to offer and carried it with them wherever they went. *Imagine that . . . and thank you Agod, was it ever refreshing.* They had narrowly escaped ruin and, somehow, made it through.

Ligatus was running into people like him often now, travelers, men and women on journeys and an expression of character that he rarely saw in recent years, but had prevailed in earlier times, independent thinkers. It had been so entirely freeing, the collapse of capitalism. America was still bountiful and beautiful, but her population had dwindled, it was absolutely necessary if the world was to survive to reduce the world's population, and those who had made it through understood this.

An older couple strolled about, not quite withered, still able to walk, and the gentle man required a cane. He wore a straw hat with a feather stuck in it and his pony-tailed hair hung down his back and his gentle lady held onto his arm. It was an interesting fact that survivors were largely individuals, not members of a herd. Only those who could think for themselves had managed to survive. Gentle man had a walking stick, and needed it.

The couple sat in an auto without a top, in America's paradise, in an antique auto originally constructed without a top and went nowhere and all dressed up they took a little trip through Pahayokee, a new idea for them but in reality a trip they had often took in another time. Past was present, right here, before them. Many things in this world were interchangeable and for these two past and present were a couple of them.

A rhythm of cardinals surrounded him and a character he had heard of but never met walked up the road to meet him. Cotteeman, 400-year-old Cotteeman, who had died yesterday but lived today on some tangential plane, was here, crossing his path.

Hey you, why you startled me. Why, hello there. Ligatus laughed. *I thought it was something stirring in the bush had made me jump, but of course, it's you.*

He laughed again. He was concerned that whatever was in the bush was as frightened as he was and he had jumped and backed off fast. These animals were so afraid of people, they didn't like to be near them and when disturbed darted very quickly back into the bush and hid.

Birds were up and at it. Cotteeman asked Ligatus a question that was a trap, one cloaked in judgement, a question formulated and posed to him with the purpose of catching him, judging him, and putting him in a word trap. He thought about this, and remembered what Greet Withe had said to Caren Shilland, never, never answer a question that is a trap, a trap to bait you and catch you - don't answer.

Ligatus and Cotteeman sat under a live oak and across from them the tall pines and scrub pines shaded and sheltered yellow-colored warblers and black and white warblers and those notorious red-bellied woodpeckers, with the red heads. Ligatus felt at home and was in good company, but hadn't slept at all last night and was subdued well into late morning. A kite flew over their heads, they believed it was a kite, *it's behaving like a kite and what a bird!* It was dragging a banner that read: **Welcome to the Parkland Way, Another Way.**

A butterfly or moth fluttered about, seemingly aimless, but headed into the nearby woodland into some unknown place, out of sight. Ligatus said he ought to follow this yellow butterfly and Cotteeman agreed. Ligatus had kept its symbolism in his head for so long now and when he was overwhelmed and saw the little guys he slowed down and followed them into the forest. In fact, he was known to follow purple moths and white ones too for months at a time.

Cotteeman said, *Yes, they will try and discredit you. They will try and win back their power and ask you a question whose answer will disgrace you.*

Ligatus mounted up and followed the moth and Cotteeman got back up on his life's path.

America's paradise had fed most of its people for so very long now, accommodating cattle and orange groves, and lots of RV parks filled with refugees escaping the northern cold. Early expeditions baptized and bestowed this place with descriptive and ancient literary and biblical names like Venus and Arcadia and nearby La Belle but in Immokalee pickers there had picked and picked as fast as they could for the past hundred years in America's Garden of Eden, its origin and paradise . . . Oh, if only people would think about it this way and were not out shopping in strip malls for everything mock could buy.

Invaders proceeded to build sewers, filling them with nearly every living thing, floating tissues and organs, killed or destroyed, cesspools and tanks topped by over-consuming types and spectators whose lives weren't in motion. So much of the living had been flushed down a toilet out into the sea. Ligatus didn't want anything to do with that, *please . . . no . . . oh my Agod.*

So many pooped on everything they touched, they squatted and grunted and strained and pooped out excrement wherever they went and wherever they wanted, and with greedy hands reached for more and shoved whatever would fit in their mouths and, still squatting, when that wasn't enough they befouled people and destroyed them and befouled places and destroyed them too. Nice bunch, and while their poop piled high, in coils, like snakes, curling high, in piles, it reached up and bit them where it hurt.

And don't ever forget, Ligatus, the ones who try hard to discredit you the most are the biggest poopers of all.

At the parkland a young girl knew where the scrub jay nested and called the jay out into the open for a glimpse. *Crisp crisp crisp crisp*, Ligatus heard her call and jay flew out and revealed itself and, just as it seemed no one else saw, above it he heard *caracaracaracaracaracara*, and an exotic looking bird flew by, undulating and singing *caracaracaracara.*

A woman stood nearby, on the edge of paradise, in front of an easel. She was painting. She looked southward over Florida Bay, with her back to paradise, and on her canvas, white pelican and pink flamingo flocked together off the coast of Cape Sable. She turned around . . . she had heard it too. Ligatus stood nearby, on his path, watching her . . . and waited.

Chapter 24

"Aw, c'mon . . . sanctioned and shunned because she wears a floral printed shawl?" Kodia asked in disbelief.

"Reviled, peed on and pooped on because she wears a folk art shawl?"

"Aw, c'mon, Geela, give me a break."

But it was the truth.

Bella Medvedetsa traveled all the way from Russia with a warning: The ice has melted at the North Pole and the bears were stranded and white bear must be moved to the South Pole, where the ice could be thicker . . . for a while anyway . . . if they were to trick death and survive.

"Only those who adapt will survive Albedo," Bella said to Kodia. "Snow cover reflects radiation, but open water absorbs it, Kodia, and Albedo has melted away the snow and ice so very fast and caused the globe to warm up even faster that I'm afraid for the bears."

"Maybe white bear will make good friends with penguin, and learn to hunt penguin way."

"It's possible . . . I suppose . . . anything is possible," Kodia mused.

The ocean to the north was the shortest route between North America and Russia and it had lost its permafrost and it was open now for sea travel twelve months a year. The sea route round the north of Canada and Alaska was clear of ice, and whales with dorsals could swim it year-round. Bowheads with no dorsals had always traveled easily under the ice but other whales with dorsals had been denied passage when ice was present.

It was governments that fostered enmity, not people. Governments, well, they must get along with the rest of the world and not take too much, if they are to survive.

"There are many people besides you Americans who live along the Circle, and we all get along: Canadians, Inuit, Kalaallit, Russians, Norwegians, Karelo-Finnish, Swedes, Sami, to name a few, and they're all my relatives," said Bella.

"Governments shouldn't bully people," was the last thing she said before she turned around and hopped back to Russia across the few pieces of remaining, floating ice.

Bella Medvedesta found Kodia sitting on a stump, wearing the same kind of shawl she wore. *Oh my*, thought Bella, *she's my relative.* Bella told Kodia that the remaining ice was melting so fast and ocean temperatures warming so quickly that Agod must move the white bears to the South Pole, and fast, if they were to survive.

Kodia believed Bella and knew it to be true. She tumbled down the hillside towards the sea, and sliding down slopes covered in tangly old growth, crashed through bushes and trees, her white shock of hair trying hard to keep up. Her flowered, folk art shawl flapped and flew on the wind and bushes grabbed pieces of it as she flew by. Those in boats off the coast watched her as she plunged down hills towards the sea, she was such a sight, and they told everyone they knew Kodia was on the move, making her a household name discussed around kitchen tables all over the land.

She quickly swam across the Salish Sea and on up the Fraser River, walked the portage to White Tents, and gave message to Geela.

"How will we get them there?" Geela asked.

"Theocean will help, he is shaman to the way north and will know what to do," replied Kodia.

"He'll use kayaks in the boggy areas then commandeer freight trains somewhere south of the bogs, where the earth firms up. He'll pack freezer cars with saltwater and ice, whatever is needed, and transport the bears by rail through the interior, all the way to the Inka Highway."

"It will be tricky, and dangerous. Tossherrheim and his goons will try and interfere."

Kodia was Kodiak bear. She lived north of the Happy People with giant, mammoth sunflowers, animated flowers who lived their lives as men, women and children, accompanying Kodia wherever she went . . . they were good company.

A wild mop of white and gray hair lay upon the colorfully designed floral shawl that draped over her shoulders. She had adapted to the way of the invaders, just like the first people had . . . and she liked a pipe too. Kodia had had men, lots of them: it was all about the tail, and she knew it, but she was retired now, living the life of a contemplative woman and she had made the trip down from the north to see for herself what all the hubbub was about, when America declined, and all that.

Kodia had swam and swam, floating across the gulf and, dragging her bulk from the water near the Columbia River, ate a lot of salmon and got right back in, for another swim. She had to get to White Tents. She had to see Agod and Geela and ask them what the heck was going on. As she traveled over the land, fiery canyon raptors, red-shouldered ones raised in the refugee camps in the south, flew overhead, out of their range. They were hunting bush meat, always circling, always hunting, hungry hunters overhead and underfoot, with many, many mouths to feed.

Where had all the money come from? Kodia asked. *Wasn't it Geronimo or someone like him who once asked that same question about the invaders? Where did they all come from, and why did there have to be so many of them?*

I want to know, where did all the money come from? And why was there so much of it? And how did the global elites and bankers get it all? How did mock and credit work? How did the elites get control of everything? How did they get so much and steal the country out from under us?

Why, the country had a printing press is how, Geela had responded, and soon enough it became so clear, couldn't be any clearer . . . really.

Very few had way more than most. And how did they do it? Mock printed out of thin air could only be used to buy assets the super rich owned, financial assets, and the super rich got all the expanded mock supply, dollars that were marked as debt for a class of serfs to repay. And what did the super rich do with it all?

The super rich created asset classes out of everything they didn't yet own: water, air, land, timber, minerals, fossil fuels, fish, electro-magnetic fields, the sun, planets, people . . . yes, people . . . and securitized them all. Globalists took possession of and aggregated assets that belonged to the earth, belonged to all of us, heck were us, and sold them to the super rich who had all the expanding mock supply . . . remember . . . funded by the mushrooming public debt. *Are you still with me, Kodia?*

Ordinary people did not have access to expanded mock, but had to pay back the debt it created, for generations, far into the future, into perpetuity. The super rich, in effect, created an asset class out of people, arbitraged their futures, their prosperity, and put them on a road to serfdom. The super rich ruled the world, and while most had become serfs, a handful of rich became the biggest aristocratic class on the planet, controlling everything and everyone . . . until it all went to crap.

And I'm not kidding, said Agod. The government printed mock and more mock and pimped and whored its people, arbitraging their standard of living, creating a class of super rich who ruled the world, for a while. But, in reality, it was fake, and in the end, worthless.

Bella was from the other side of the sea, a young woman from Russia, and Kodia's cousin, but reviled by the corporatist class. Who does she think she is? Corporatists resented her message from the other side of the sea and persisted in cultivating enmity, through the media and political classes. My Agod, what a way to run a world! She was peed on and pooped on because she wore a colorful, floral printed dress – sanctioned and shunned for the sake of a market place.

Kodia sat on a stump and tended a campfire—the day without wind, a quiet morning, but cold enough for snow—and she moved slowly about her campground. Long white and gray hair grew from her head and was woven into tapestry that sat snug against a colorfully designed shawl that lay on her shoulders.

Kodiak Island was north of where the Happy People lived and, along with giant, mammoth sunflowers, Kodia lived there contentedly, just like survivors lived with the sequoias, happily. It was something about flowers that tugged at her heart, and happy was good. Wrapped in a colorful shawl she wore its flowers on her shoulders, and a gray shock of hair. Giant animated sunflowers were her friends and entourage and she traveled everywhere with them. Checkered white-tailed dragon flies and their damsels were sentinel, and hovered overhead.

She loved to dance, Kodia was a bear that loved to dance, a dancing bear . . . maybe with some Russian heritage. She always wore the same colorful shawl. Her sunflowers animated and lived lives as women, men and children, and were good, pleasant company for Kodia, nicely complementing her extra-ordinary way of life.

In a contemplative mood, she sensed, somehow intuited, a distant approach from another, faraway land. The air cooled down fast. Sitting on the other side of the sea, she put on a wool cap and pulling her shawl close, waited.

Advent stirred, and this dawn of another day knew not what followed would bring. Awakening swelled, but still no sound. Then, up above, on another ridge, quiet snapped and faint tremor rumbled and rolled from a distant, other side of the sea.

Noise began and crashed, it was loud in the now nearby forest. Bella Medvedetsa was running, rolling, falling, stumblishly skidding and slipping down slopes, breaking branches and trees while she charged as fast as she could along the ridge, and as she ran little bits of her shawl, the flowers of Russia, snagged on bushes and shrubs and low branches. She fell through the timber in search of Kodia, her relative, and stopped short, out of breath.

The snow, it was not heavy, the sky and ocean were smoky and white. Little bits of green moved across the ocean in suprasessive shades of gray. There was color in the nearby houses, then gray came again with little bits of green and Kodia pulled back her hair and listened to the wind and ocean while they lie down, and were quiet.

Hundreds of black-winged birds moved through the forest with shallow dips and dives, perambulating from one tree limb to another, to one limb, then the next. Silently they moved, like snowflakes they fell, halting and moving as one in the snow covered trees while gray, brown, white, green, and blue peeked through.

These colors required light, without it couldn't be seen and in the low light her bright, yellow, wooly winter hat, the one her mother had made, banded, but was subdued in the orchestrally, dim-lit light.

If Bella can't see it, she won't find me.

After the gentle storm, the day after the storm and the night after the storm, the snow stayed in the trees, and in the heavy wood it felt like a cave, dense and close. Then snow began to drop and fall and melted advent's ambiance away.

"I've been looking for you, cousin," Bella stopped short, shouting from breathless lungs. "I swam and swam and ran and ran . . . all the way from Russia." Bella was a young dancing bear from across the sea and was wearing a printed dress and apron made of colored floral cloth. She was Kodia's relative.

The Arctic Ocean was hugely significant. Once the ice melted it was the shortest route between North America and Russia. The passage had been a legendary sea route around the north of Canada and Alaska and was clear of ice now, all year round. Bowhead whale had no dorsal fin and could easily travel under the ice but killer whales had dorsals and previously couldn't, but now ice has melted and they've migrated northward – only the animals that adapt will survive.

So Kodia, a bear from Kodiak, living out the days of her life, swam the sound again, this time to warn Agod of the grim circumstances the polar bears faced. Kodia brought message to Geela and Geela, with the help of many others in the Wilderness League, organized a train ride and moved the white bears to Antarctica. They were transported by kayak till they hit solid ground, south of the bogs, then put in freight cars. Canadian geese escorted the company into the interior and white pelican took over considerably south of north.

Women in the north knitted with needles belonging to their grandmothers, knitting needles were their inheritance. Kodia got hers from her grandmother when she died, but forgot how she came by them. Had her mother given them to her or had her grandmother, just before she died?

These northern women knitted their dreams, dumb dreams that couldn't speak, and the women worked them into knitting or drawing or sculpture, and story, and in the Arctic, where the future of the world lay, so many dreams didn't translate into words, they absolutely didn't translate into words, and dumb Kodia and dumb Bella found other ways to tell dumb dreams.

Kodia's mind didn't work well in reverse, to quote her father. There was a reason why your mother knitted hats, told story and made art, if not, the dream or story would slip into a deep, dark pool, and become hard to retrieve. It required a big effort when dreams sank deep into dark pools . . . one not many liked to make: dive deep and retrieve; an arduous journey, but it was important work.

Kodia became like the mute women who knitted and after inquiring in what language one dreamed, modeled it for those whose senses had atrophied. After all, everyone was capable of journeying like shamans and men and women everywhere began to travel again in shaman-like way.

After it snowed, and four or five feet of snow fell, there was still no wind in the woods. She walked around and snow crunched under her feet. In the late afternoon the trees were still wearing snow, on their trunks and branches, stretching all the way to the tips of their needles and here in the woods, a snow cave was created, limiting her field of vision.

Sigh. *Not much sunlight, very little of it really,* she said to herself and as she crunched the snow underfoot it squeaked. A little light, diffused light, illuminated the bluish-white sun ball in the late afternoon winter sky, and it was beautiful, but hard walking.

She was out of breath but then she had had a respiratory problem for so long now− another reason why she had retired. She sighed again.

She felt like an old grandmother walking through the woods looking for a place to sit down and die. It was her respiratory problem making her feel that way, walking through these low limbs heavy with snow, but it just wasn't cold enough to freeze to death and die.

If it was colder it could happen really fast and be a perfect way to go. If not she would dive into the serpentine green color along a pacific shore and drown, if she could find the courage.

The trees were squeaking wet and caught her attention. Birds sang *and that white isn't blue, it is yellow,* she thought.

Magic and the snow put weight upon things in the forest, and patches of briar were shaped into little canopies and caves, formed by snow, bent low into little rooms with roofs, created by snow. Pine branches were heavy, bowed low and touched the ground. In other places smaller shrubs and saplings began to lose their weight and, springing back, bounced and nodded in an animated fashion. She liked it, and was glad.

Another little world existed inside the snow caves and she crawled in and sat down and spoke with Agod. Heris was under the canopy playing his and her violin, and with her and his ear to the ground, listened to the earth sounds, and the wind as it picked up and hit the earth and screamed through the woods and trees and forest, and caves. It was the breath of Agod, and Agod was so mad and disappointed with people, Agod took away cold and turned up the heat.

Kodia saw this in a dream, before it all happened, as did Bella. She had come all the way from Russia to obey her dream. *Reality? What's that?*

On a mountain top Kodia was skiing down, down, down, but didn't know where she was going. She was in the woods, in the mountains, on the snow, in the winter and saw small shrubs and many branches covered with snow. She sniffled and snorted snot back into her nasal chamber as she wandered and skied over snow. Green was gone, only white remained, white and black, white with black lines sketching white leaves, elongated needles stretched and exaggerated by snow: green gone now but black and white remained. There was a little world in there, underneath that space, the space that had been created by snow and it was a very good, little place.

Photograph me with my sunflowers in the snow, just before I die . . . please.

Kodia was photographed, her last photograph in the snow, with her sunflowers growing through the snow, just before she died. Her flowers *podsnezhnikom,* death heralded, the portrait drawn . . . and she was gone.

She had stung and, like the honey bee, must die.

Chapter 25

The northern sea route was clear of ice now and people living along the Circle did not embrace the enmity governments had fostered, but cooperated with one another and modeled a right attitude for the whole, remaining world. The polars desperately wanted to survive Albedo, and it would take a world effort to achieve this, so, for Agod's sake, people must get along and get on board.

Theocean lived as shaman in the way north, in the region of the North Pole, and used his bag of tricks to get things done. It fell on him to use his power and move white bear to the south, where penguin would teach white bear to hunt south-pole way – otherwise bear would eat penguin. Theocean saw his power and announced kayaks and freight trains would come and take polar bear to Antarctica and Geela would fly to the North Pole and accompany the caravan all the way to the South Pole.

Crisp, cold soundlessness broke as geese flew overhead, honking noisily and invading the airspace. The geese were friendly and ferocious members of the Wilderness League, good allies to have, and in colder months the honkers fed in the lower states and for the privilege provided good intelligence on the Arctic Circle.

Theocean looked up at them and sensed it was time to leave. He had been staring for a long time at an unattractive plant growing nearby before he gently tugged and pulled the weed for a closer look. Its root looked a little like a person, but more closely resembled the antlers of an antelope, or elk. It animated underground. The plant was pollinated by wind, its flowers too ordinary to attract insects. Its redolence faintly reminded him of something, but he knew not what. It was knotted and threadlike, and its tiny roots changed elements from the soil into visionary pathways, and Theocean dove deep, journeyed deep, and asked plant intelligence what the heck was going on and what the heck ought he be doing about it.

He shook the plant and a woman met him at a portal. Her feet looked like chicken claws, her toenails curled into crispy, crusty swirls. She was ugly and as she sallied forth among tumbling leaves, ashen in color, some with gray in them, their sun washed color dusted the air, blurring her surrounds. About her, all the houses had hearts and souls and were animated. Theocean was a little like this woman with chicken claws for feet, for when light retrenched and dimness rose he ran for cover in the underworld, and looked for answers there.

The hair on her shins grew all the way down to her feet and it was shaggy and intertwined with the hair growing on her big toes, and she wore it in plaits.

I would have burned your house down but it had a heart and soul, she said as she brushed passed him, pushing him aside. *I ought to throw you around this place, Theocean, like a wet rag doll. In fact, I think I will.*

The woman with the chicken feet was walking fast, she was enormous, and as she took strides the fat on first one thigh thrust forward, ahead of her, one thigh always in the way of the other, and rubbing together, created friction, and in this way she advanced.

Take this, she held up a plant, *and everything in your way will get out of your way. Take it. It will allow your people, your gendarmes, to steer the great trees, Sequoia and Greylock, and deliver the bears through all obstacles, on their way to the South Pole,* she said to Theocean and he took the herb from her hand.

The underground place was pretty and the sun was shining. It looked a lot like parkland and many people were there, survivors, living the parkland way, but in animated houses with hearts and souls.

The enormous woman was young and as she strode along the avenue the sandals on her feet sounded *flip-flop flip-flop* and her feet angled outwards, spraddling away from her sides. Theocean had never seen her before. She was overweight, seemingly self-conscious but wait, not really, only detached, detached from her body, not in it. She wore a disguise and when she advanced created great energy while her perambulators endeavored to walk their own way, on another path.

She strolled along on a road very few knew, in a young woman's disfigured figure, grotesque really, from too much neglect, and only Agod knew why. There were no sidewalks, as the road did not accommodate pedestrians. Cars sped past and as she stepped along without the protection of a safe foot path, because there was no clear walkway, she was involved in dialogue, talking to herself. Her large chin extended and seemed to argue with another self and at other times, tucking her chin inwards and downwards, seemed, occasionally, in agreement, and agreeing, soothed and stroked an inner self.

Theocean strained hard but couldn't hear everything that was discussed between the two, whether inner agreed or not, because he was hiding now, lying low behind a wall. From the other side her voice and the sounds it made, its sighs and arousals, didn't penetrate the wall nor rise over the top of the low wall and settle downwards, but approached him obtusely and drifted obliquely from around a corner and coming at him nudged his shoulder and asked permission before entering his ear. Theocean was soon exhausted, took a drink and quickly fell asleep.

A swift river thundered by, and Theocean found its quiet pool and took a bath. The nearby rocks were slippery and because he had had some bourbon, didn't want to walk on slippery rocks. But pool . . . pool . . . there was that and he splashed and bathed and when he finished, walked up the trail he entered by but slipped on running-fast river's bank and bounced backwards one, two, three, right, left, right over rocks and ripped a bush and snapped and broke its branches on the way down, landing on a rock. It should have hurt but it felt like he had hit a feather bed.

At another threshold a tree frog jumped out in front of him onto a birch and, scaling, climbed like a spider. It had fantastically splayed feet and bulbous toes and climbed like a spider till it reached a certain height and then it was Cotteeman, 400-year-old Cotteeman, climbing like tree frog scampered.

A woman in a loose cotton shift and a sweater draped over her shoulder was wearing rubber boots on her feet, loose around the calf and, turning to look at him while continuing to walk, moved away at an angle not in front nor behind, but askant, towards slanting rows of patterns whose colors were not the same.

Water had its own shade and when Theocean opened his eyes, a cormorant was posted at the edge of the pool, perched upright on a pink granite shoulder, wearing a red, gauzy handkerchief over its eyes. It beckoned him. He looked quickly around and saw only a child swimming nearby. Excitedly and in a hushed tone he said to the child, "Look at that queer bird. Do you see it?" But the boy, singing and splashing, paid no heed.

Theocean was curious and swam over to the cormorant and lifted off its mask and the slender-bodied bird was able to see again, and grunted and gave its thanks and then using its hooked bill, clung tightly to Theocean's arm, and Theocean and the cormorant swam around the pool in the running-fast river together for several days.

Then Theocean turned towards the bird and sàid, "I don't understand. You are a great swimmer and fisherman. I have often watched you dive into the water and resurface with a squirming fish only to casually flip it into the air and devour it head-first. Why are you hanging onto me?"

The bird replied, "No longer do I want to dive and fish for my supper. I want you to catch it for me. If only you allow me to continue my clutch upon you I can teach you how to be a great fisherman too."

Well, Theocean had often watched cormorant from the edge of the river and witnessed all cormorant could do upon the water's surface and thought it a splendid idea to learn what the cormorant did below, and he agreed. He quickly learned to float with his body submerged so only his head and neck were visible above water, and this skill proved to be ideal for the rather quick dives he needed to make from the surface, when the shadows of fish flickered by.

After his lessons, cormorant ordered Theocean to collect sticks in the great heat to line the nest that cormorant kept in a leafless, dead, old oak tree. The cormorant behaved like a lazy, entitled person might, and mostly sat around all day, sending Theocean off with the other cormorants on communal fishing trips. Together the birds lined up along the edge of the river and, moving towards the opposite bank thrashed their wings, driving the smaller fish into shallow water. This was hard work for Theocean for he had to fight the larger, greedier birds for a trout of his own, and yet another for the lazy, entitled one with the gauze over its head.

Back in the nest, the lazy one put its handkerchief back on its head and preferred to snack in the shade, but with its eyes on, and closed. For awhile Theocean was contented. He found clams clinging to the undersides of rocks and speared a crawling creature with his own, now sharp, hooked bill. But above, the lazy, entitled one, with its back to Theocean, preened and, with its wings wide open, worshipped the sun. The hedonist in it loved to feel the heat of the sun upon its slick, gleaming, oily, black feathers as it looked upon its well-lined nest in its leafless, dead, old oak tree.

When Theocean woke, he desired to wrest himself free from the bird's grip and, twisting violently, freed himself and returned to the others, still there in the pool swimming, splashing and laughing. He tried hard to ignore, to forget the cormorant slowly sinking behind him but looking up saw the woman who earlier had worn a loose cotton shift but was now wearing a white linen dress, and pointing with her eyes. Beneath her in the shade of the pool a faint, dark shadow drifted downward, and Theocean dove again past the river's surface.

Under the water with his eyes open, he glimpsed the fowl floating downwards, feet first, its long, orange throat in a lifeless stretch and as the bird's body sank to the river's bottom Theocean dove deeper for a closer look. He had to be sure and cupping his hands around cormorant's weightless body, Theocean guided it upwards towards the day and surface, lifting the bird out of the deep pool and into the air. A stream of water poured from its mouth – the bird was finally dead and gone, at long last dead and gone.

Next Theocean took some time and walked along a trail which followed the running-fast river. It was densely populated with spectators, a place where many went to view the wildlife. Theocean typically steered clear of spectators, they were a pain in the neck really, but he was having a good day and decided to take this little walk.

Theocean thought, *I'd like a little shack here along this running-fast river and have the place to myself. Holy mackerel would I like that.*

The cormorants were tame and had little green eyes with dials around them, graduated and marked like a compass. In the center of green was a black pupil and, of course, with orange all over, those black feathers, those gorgeously textured, nuanced, iridescent little black feathers in the orange and green, glimmered, and anyone could grab one by the neck and stick it in a bag and put it to work.

Then, of course, he knew what the redolence of the plant had suggested and shook loose in him, an evocative knowing of superpower's soft power imposing oppression without anyone really noticing.

He would really, really like to have a place to himself along this fast moving river to watch those in the pool splash and play and have fun, and watch the wild creatures too, the exquisite ones and survivors, and rest. But those with gauzy, red kerchiefs on their heads had lost their way and were making a mess of things. Their nests were lined with feathers from other birds' nests, birds not yet born, and when they stretched their wings out over the land they made serfs out of anyone, anyone they could grab by the neck. Theocean left the river bank and knew what he had to do, his little part for the greater good, to help set-up a bigger good.

Years ago white bear had tried to swim to Antarctica, but perished, and the other ones the bears who stayed behind began to mate with the browns and the grizzlies, and eat gopher and other things instead of seal, and by assimilating, they altered their genetics and evolved and learned to live off-ice. Still, others yearned to live the old way, but with the loss of permafrost, the South Pole was the only viable alternative, and as it remained frozen, or so they thought, many were willing to risk the trip and give it a go. Theocean insisted bear ride in kayaks and canoes – he did not want to lose anymore bear and the whales, well, any whales wishing to make the journey could easily swim and meet bear there.

When Geela arrived, they set off. She flew out in front of the caravan of kayaks and canoes as it made its way southward through the northern bogs. Their friends watched as they paddled away and it broke their hearts and some jumped in the sea and tried to swim the length of the globe to be with them. Northern peoples living along the Circle and others, wild animals and birds and muskox, all wanted to go with white bear to the South Pole, and not be left behind, but had to find their own way through the boggy earth to the railheads and catch the train to the South Pole.

Theocean transported thousands of bears in kayaks and canoes and his slow, meandering water caravan made its way to a freight depot deep inside the interior, during a peak solar explosion, so they would not be detected.

The Arctic was in an advanced melting state and believe it or not a train ride from the north to the south poles made good sense. The rail lines in North America were still intact, the roads, too, for that matter, and the Inka Highway, well, it had survived some 25,000 years. *Some things last and some things pass*, Geela said . . . and she commandeered trains and trucks and rails and whatever else was necessary to get the bears to the South Pole, upsetting the corporatists in the process.

They left the winter north and traveled at a pace that allowed for an arrival, in the winter south, in six months' time. But mine owners and frackers and extractors still used these transportation routes to move minerals and fossil fuels and hired Tossherrheim and his goons to stop any interruption in their business affairs and before Theocean could implement his plan, Tossherrheim decided to slaughter the remaining bears. He didn't like all the photos in the newspapers—front page, top fold—of bear floating in temperate-zoned swimming pools. He wanted no living sign of bears' struggle or obvious proof of global warming so it was disguised as a massacre, a massacre of necessity by those living a subsistence lifestyle at the Circle. But people living on the Circle refused to play along. They liked the idea of moving bear instead. This plan had hope . . . bear might one day return. After all, global temperatures were beginning to drop now, were they not, and they foiled Tossherrheim's plan, the people of the north, where the future of the whole world lay, because they really, really didn't like the likes of Tossherrheim.

Tossherrheim failed. He didn't manage to murder the bears at the Pole and targeted Panama instead for his final attack. In Panama he tried again to take out the Wilderness League. There he fabricated an identity and was sure he could count on the Isthmians to do his dirty work.

A dirty woman sat near a black shallow pool that was coated in pollen, wearing gray clothes and gray dirt and gray hair and gray skin. The pool had no light value. She held a stick in her hand and with it drew encrypted story in the pollen dust collected on the pool's surface and pushing it around, tried to show others the way. She hid her face behind her gray hair but her lips were visible and constantly moving. In her movie she spoke in tongues to herself, translating and recasting all. Her sneakers were laced up tightly and dirty. Her hands and her nails carried soil and someone looking like her walked over to where she sat and stood next to her and watched her speak and draw while she spoke in a language of many tongues. Yes, and when she passed her friend remained and drew story and carried the conversation alone.

She lived in the boats on the Great Lakes, this lady in gray clothes and while she drew messages in pollen dust, a great blue heron waded along the reedy end of one of the lakes, stepping through the warm shallow water where pickerel weed grew. Along its edge blueberry bush had taken root, heavy with large, blue beauties. The bird stretched its neck and craning plucked at the plump morsels then stopped a moment and turning inside itself shuddered and shook, its feathers flicking and flinging water in swirls of loose, wide arcs and arching its neck backwards screeched in total ecstasy. Outside this sphere of lady in gray and heron, woodpecker drilled and hammered and *tapped tapped tapped* the gray lady's stories and her message resonated and reverberated in the thudding dull quiet of forest, bouncing and echoing off glacial outcrops . . . *thunk* . . . *thunk* . . . *thunk* . . . received and heard by only those living Another Way.

The color of the light was gray then it brightened and infused white light into oak trunks, then white oak vibrated in still warm air in autumn time, a diffused sun on an angle in a late western sky. Diffused rays of light scattered through dense clouds and up on over the lakes into a vibrating, pulsing, pleurisy of gray and swam around in her head and permeated her brain. In dreamtime the light of storm approached and she dreamed storm and tornadoes darkened the skies and earth.

Geela received her power from where? Her life's journey, she supposed. *I've translated all that I know, and have learned, and realigned my knowledge with experience, and the collective unconsciousness, and . . . of course . . . Agod.*

Theocean woke to a circle of thunderstorms about his camp. He was standing in the center of a clear pool.

Chapter 26

The ants crossed the Colorado and made it to California and watered the crops. Along the way they struggled, dragging hose with the constant fear of being destroyed or starved to death and once or twice they lost their queen and made new ones but in the end prevailed.

Safely on the other side, Wishtonwish left them, the ants and Ptarro, and returned to Dakota. He had much work to do. The fracking shafts needed deep cleaning; too much pollution and contamination had poisoned the water in under the ground wells. Remedy was required, and he faced obstacles and obstructionists ahead.

Wishtonwish trotted along a frozen trail. Each slap of his paw struck an echo that reverberated in a hollow, cave-like space between snow and ice, far ahead along the path. First it had snowed, and then sleet fell on top of the snow. After sleet stopped and the late December afternoon temperature began to climb, it warmed up then plummeted, forming a crust, a tough outer crust with soft snow inside, like a baguette, and the hollow sounds between snow and ice rebounded and, trotting the dog, rang story.

Wishtonwish was running on snow and it surprised him. Only yesterday he had had to struggle through it, to trudge through heavy snow. It sure was easier going this way and under his feet the added depth lent height to a view he would have otherwise never seen. He could walk on top of twisted briar patches and tangly undergrowth and see areas otherwise inaccessible, like soggy northern Canada in warm season.

It was a good day, the wind howled in his ear and he was already in Nebraska. Black snow fleas jumped ahead, crawling and hopping along the snowy trail and heralded his other approach. Wishtonwish saw a young stag with wide antlers last night in dreamtime, leaping and running and chasing after many does. His ancestors had walked and rode on frozen tundra, using snow shoes and sleds and, later, motorized vehicles. They had had access because it was frozen, not unfrozen, and migrated to places otherwise inaccessible, by way of ice and cold. They traversed on mountain tops, not over them, and lakes and canyon so deep it was almost unimaginable.

As snow melted, the ice melted, revealing distinct tiers of decomposing debris and earth. Layers of wind swept limb and branch and twig and leaf off and away, and tops of mountains and buried lakes slowly emerged through evaporated snow, laid in winter on high-latitudinal Arctic plains. Those in the unseen lands knew Wishtonwish was coming, a bouncing echo announced his arrival.

Frost visited and drew an ice palace in a mountain range covered with tilted conifers, wind-tilted conifers, then snow collapsed, beautifully etching high drifts of powder packed in valleys and peaks. The air above was still and the limbs on trees and outer twigs stretched and reached the sky. Nearby, North America's great, old grandmother lay in repose and woke. She rose up out of the ground and inhaled ever so softly, ever so lightly. The tree tops hardly moved and her breath barely stirred but ever so lightly, and softly, their tops jingled and tinkled like bells and when she exhaled ice formed and coated the branches, and froze them a while.

During this time the sun stood still, like a slack tide. Moon light rose in wintry skies. The atmosphere was white-washed and lightly diffused; trees stood still and held their breaths and waited and not a breath of air was breathed for a very long time. Wishtonwish walked along this twilight road and cold, sharp wafts of wind filled his lungs. An owl flew out from the wood, crossed the road in front of him, and perched on a hawthorn tree just as silently as the wind that didn't stir stirred that night. A dog barked and the owl flew away.

He went to work. Wishtonwish and friends monitored under the ground water quality, clearing the shafts, fracking arteries and tar pits of all poison and while cleaning they found piles and piles of gold and acres and acres of stacked dollar bills, some with serial numbers that had never circulated and others simply withdrawn from circulation. Thousands of paintings were there, too, stashed when the West's version of capitalism pooped out.

The dogs used the mock to line their burrows and keep the cold out. They had no use for gold but thought it beautiful and built mounds and temples above the ground with it and hung the paintings on the temple walls, but continued to harvest nuts and seeds.

Unpublished bank accounts stretched for miles and miles and Geela did not recognize the serial numbers but Theocean did and cracked the code. Theocean had told Wishtonwish where to look for the mock and gold and art stored underground; he had seen it all, while he was under another ground on his quest for guidance.

While workers ran in circles panting like dogs, mock had been circulated by way of binary code, making serfs out of most.

"The mock we found was stashed by the elites," Wishtonwish told the other prairie dogs, "to take with them to a new world. The paper trail, the unpublished accounts, climbed like Jacob's ladder to a new world but Agod stopped them and made them come back to the this old earth and reckon with us survivors, and the rest of the world."

"All the mock circulated and recirculated in secrecy, binary code manipulated by the super rich with the same fervor desperate people played at gambling games, ceased to be, and the bankers and elites no longer controlled the world and people thrived again, and lived Another Way."

"You see, bankers made mock out of everything, and from nothing. They didn't handle mock physically, or print much of it at all. They didn't have to. They expanded it using electrical impulse, and created the illusion of wealth."

Zeros and ones were about as physical as it got for these guys, binary code being the physical stuff. Bankers arranged the code into ordered groups and the code that controlled the mock supply was manipulated to benefit only the elite – and the larger the mock supply became the less most had of it, naturally. Bankers controlled extraordinary amounts of mock and as its supply increased exponentially, using zeros and ones, bankers increasingly controlled every aspect of peoples' lives. Most became serfs and lost control of their futures and everything they owned – and their assets, wealth, labor, and income were all expropriated.

Inside central banks mock was bundled and delivered only to those who owned financial assets, using high voltage to amplify the mock supply and low voltage to deliver it into the hands of a few. The speed and efficiency with which bankers were able to concentrate wealth into the hands of a few, making serfs out of most, was extraordinary really, and with just zeros and ones, and the cherry on top, bankers marked it all as debt for serfs to repay.

Then their version of capitalism failed . . .

A man skated by on rollers, and in a great hurry. He was wearing a latex body suit printed with an American flag motif and shouted, "Someone is coming to bury Wishtonwish alive, and fast. Quick, do something."

Tossherrheim saw everything and all the sparkling gold and fine art had caught his eyes, leading him to Wishtonwish and his dogs. He sent his goons to trap Wishtonwish in a fracking shaft, throw him and his dogs deeper still inside a vein, seal its entrance, kill them and take all that glittered was gold.

Caren Shilland was sentry and guarded the entrance to the underground shafts. The dogs had gone to ground but on this particular day Caren was distracted, trying to convince the Cold People to help Wishtonwish and his prairie dogs clean the shafts. Caren was working the Cold People, working them hard, but Cold People, the squatters who lived nearby and liked central heat, wouldn't help out. Oh, she tried hard to persuade them to help Wishtonwish and live Another Way, but they were scared and not sure whose side they ought to be on. Still, Caren tried.

"You've run out of time," she said. "Winning isn't the goal any longer, survival is. The whole world is threatened with extinction."

"It's a little like the human experience. There is less and less time, a body has less and less time as it ages. The world as we know it has aged and there is less and less time for screwing around," Caren said.

"The stakes are high and though most think it's too late, Agod doesn't," and while trying to convince Cold People to be better people, Tossherrheim's goons got past her and into the mines.

The dogs had gone deeper yet, to ground. They ran and ran for miles and miles in supersized arteries twenty miles deep and a hundred miles wide. Through the insides of the earth, running and running through cavernous tunnels, they cleaned with brooms and tails and, scraping pollution, swept it all out. It had taken decades for them to get this far and clean as far as they had because the big machines under the ground no longer worked. Conveyor belts lay idle and couldn't carry the debris and detritus along its tracks to the surface so, moving forward then backward like only prairie dogs could, they plowed and dug deep. Digging furiously with front paws they swept what they had loosened with their back paws and, turning around, pushed like plows anything left behind.

Wishtonwish was all alone, stuck inside a shallow shaft. He wasn't able to maneuver one way or the other and with no moves left, and sick, with very little water or air, he was trapped, and nearly died. All his life Wishtonwish and his dogs were pursued by powerful forces in the world, but his people were accustomed to it and had not been stopped . . . slowed down, yes, but not stopped. As Tossherrheim wouldn't release him unless the others abandoned their efforts to clean and clear fracking shafts and give him all the gold, money, and art, Wishtonwish, sitting there, tried to figure a way out.

The moon in the sky outside was blue. Wishtonwish sat in one place rocking back and forth, trying to soothe his self. Behind him a guy, someone who was following him earlier, got close, too close, just in a neighboring channel. Another goon watched Wishtonwish through a hole in the tunnel's roof and, while it seemed he would slowly choke to death, Wish decided he needed to shake up his head, and fast. It was important.

Kick me out and kick me back in, is that it?

What can I do? he thought. *Why hurry to get back out into that world corporatists made? I hate it. My mind is stuck and, yes, I am stuck.*

When I was a youngster a bully in the neighborhood chased me through the tunnels, he wanted my very fast bicycle. He chased me and chased me and I was scared but light of foot, and fast, and I ran with my bicycle through the narrower tunnels and went down so deep the bully couldn't catch me. Yes . . . I remember and my fear was so great it almost paralyzed me but in the end it didn't, and I prevailed. Later, as I grew older, I noticed we were all chased by greedy guys who wanted what we had. They tried hard to corner and trap us and work us to death, and often succeeded, but somehow we survived, didn't we?

Well, what will become of me now, trapped, like I am, in this tunnel?

Some dogs detoured through a tunnel that opened to a way out but a great force was waiting to push them back in. Many were caught and killed and others forced back into the ground, trapped by an army sent to claim all the money and gold.

Others managed to escape and demanded something be done to help Wishtonwish. Maybe Greylock's old growth forest could rescue Wishtonwish? Or Greet's Jumping Beans? Fig Sherkin was kingfisher from Platte and Erhon Geren, green heron. They collaborated closely with Wishtonwish and knew his mind. They urged someone fetch Geela, and fast, she would know what to do.

The dogs kept the roofs of the tunnels secure and collapsed them only when an area had been thoroughly cleaned. But residual concentrations of chemical dust and gases remained behind and could be used to create an explosion so when the dogs turned off the ventilation fans . . . boom . . . up pushed the ground.

They were all so old, an army of bankers and all so old. Bankers who never died, and neither did their mock. They lived forever in walking corpses, living on and on, off zeros and ones . . . and serfs. These super rich, super old and super rich, were stripping the mounds and temples the prairie dogs built with their found gold, with their bare hands. It was all so strange and uncharacteristic of them, with their sleeves rolled up, getting their hands dirty, grabbing mock and art and then, as fast as they could, clanking away in rickety old skeletons with their hit men trailing behind, struggling to keep up because, well, it had all blown up in their face.

Several dogs had died and Tossherrheim was in a hurry to get away, particularly when Agod showed up. His minions hadn't succeeded, his mock money men had failed, and though some had managed to survive, too much fake money was chasing too few resources and, in the end, the super rich, seemingly living on and on, forever in our minds, ceased to exist.

In another part of the country Geela was on the road and experiencing trouble, somewhere near the isthmus. She really ought not go but somehow she managed a quick flight and leaving the caravan behind flew to White Tents to make a plan.

"Someone from the parklands must go to the aid of Wishtonwish," said Agod.

"No," she said, "you must go. It's time."

So Caren sent Canada's geese to fly and get Agod and escort Agod here, to Dakota, and Agod rescued Wishtonwish, as it should be, and Wishtonwish was reunited with the other dogs who had managed to survive.

Cold People saw all this and began to come around and Caren Shilland left Dakota to help with the transport of polar bears to the South Pole. Canada's geese showed her the way. Greylock was on his way too, and the Jumping Beans. Geela was having trouble in the isthmus and Jumping Beans were always willing to work, always willing to help out and didn't necessarily need to be asked.

Geela and Wreda and Greet along with Caren Shilland were all dreaming the same dream now. They were flying with Agod. Agod had resumed Agod's rightful place as leader in the Occident with all Agod's power. People looked to Agod and watched Agod and Agod looked upon and watched over people and while mortals used plant power to see forward and feel below and find the power behind the present, beyond the future, and ahead on the path, once again, Agod mattered.

There was a big party and the people were drinking and eating well. Everyone everywhere had heard the news of Wishtonwish's rescue and Agod's intervention. They had been waiting so long for this, for Agod to reveal Agod's self. The Happy People in Sequoia were partying in grand style, in only the way people who cling to trees could, as were those at the North Pole. People there turned cartwheels and made angels in the snow. But they were celebrating at a liminal time, in a liminal place, at the start, the beginning of Another Way, and many more would die yet, fighting the residual strength of the remaining elites.

Wishtonwish rested. Barred owl flew down and stood at his feet. Now, Wishtonwish loved his dogs more than anything else in the whole world, they were terrific, and when owl watered at the dogs' dish, some eyebrows were raised. But owl had a friend who told her a story and she wanted to share it with Wishtonwish. The others settled down to listen too.

Tossherrheim and Papel and Stoonman were tied to a nearby tree stump, degenerate plants, slurping and sucking and snorting for money like drug addicts pine for a fix, but without hope, and were forced to listen as well.

"Many many years ago a pair of great horned owls built a nest near a busy street, but soon destroyed it. What made owl destroy its nest, do you suppose?" owl asked Wishtonwish.

"Was it an immature owl that built its nest too close to the road? Or a naïve owl?" guessed Wishtonwish.

"Maybe, but I'm not so sure. So much of what an owl does is innate. I believe the owl was mirror."

"Some who watched the owl build its nest so close to the road were thinking the owl wanted people to see it, and perhaps had a message. They believed this particular pair of great horned owls was sent to instruct human beings."

"This, of course, was inference, one suggesting the power behind the forces of creation, the mystery of life, the mysterious light from which all life emanates, and is incomprehensible to so many."

"They built their nest where they were sure to be seen by lots, close to the road, at a busy intersection. Yes, this is the spot where they chose to build their nest, but the sanctity of it was not preserved."

"It was, largely, not the nature of Americans to preserve the sanctity of anything. The great horned owls' response to the intrusion and invasion of the god-awful spectators was to destroy the nest and kill their hatchlings."

"There was not one spectator, including my friend, who came close to matching the nobility or grace those creatures possessed. You see, the owls were intercessors Wishtonwish . . . it's an allegory . . . for one of contemporary life's important messages."

"Wildlife had become a novelty, a tourist attraction. Wildlife management? What an oxymoronic phrase."

"Americans took whatever they wanted from whomever they wanted . . . wherever and whenever they wanted. They destroyed aspects of a place and then erected monuments and named sport teams and places for whoever and whatever and wherever it was they destroyed . . . once they were safely dead and gone."

"One owl parent perched away from the nest, and watched. The other sat on it. With no sanctity, and hordes of spectators, there was nothing they could do but watch the spectre, and wait."

"The parents sensed the owlets in the nest were in extreme danger; mother was trapped and, feeling helpless, killed her offspring and only when the owls destroyed their nest and their nestlings did people leave them alone. Some understood; a message was sent to those who were paying attention . . . and they didn't like it."

"I know this feeling, I live it every day. Learn something from it."

"What are necessary are humility and wonder, awe and amazement," said Wishtonwish softly to himself.

Colder air was forced down from the pole and, after awhile, it got very cold again. Tossherrheim and his goons escaped and the struggle continued.

Chapter 27

A wind drove a rain that drove a fog that draped the land. Unfamiliar scents blew in off tropical plants and the bears were restless.

A warm, grape smell wafted muscadine over the land. This was earth of dense vegetation. A nearby marsh surrounded a point that stuck out into a southern sea – choked and concealed. The bird sanctuaries there held berries and grapes, and warblers and sparrows and rabbits and ground hogs flittered and scampered about within and, under the bush, were not seen; no wind and a still, late-night silence saturated with fog burped crickets and frogs.

Whale swam and sang off the coast in accompaniment. Whale was not racing bear to get there first, but to get there at all. It was a little like an insurance policy, really an indemnification. Some bears had to make it there, unhurt and alive, or they'd be lost forever. Whale had survived so much slaughter at the hands of men they wanted to stand with bear, and show them the way.

Where are the penguins? Are we there yet? Holy mackerel, are we not there yet?

Tugging up hill was difficult, it was so steep. Freight car doors were open for air, any air, it was so hot and stifling inside. Looking out through the open doors over towards the west, a campground emerged out of the fog, then the more distinct shapes of tents and stoves. They disappeared and the campground was gone and the train's caravan continued to chug around in a different kind of way, feeling its way, blindly now, in the fog. A woman tipped a stump of wood, an old piece of rotting wood sitting on the ground. She lifted it and quickly picked at the bugs as they crawled around, looking for cover, and she had a good meal.

Bear saw another campground with tents and stoves over to the east, and then it was gone. Like in swirling snow, they thought, watching someone disappear into the white then they were gone. Here, too, people were nomadic and their houses left with them and after passing through thousands of miles of bricks and mortar and framed houses the illusion of fog reminded bear of living in snow and inside the freight cars, the souls of bear fluttered.

Bear didn't like moving fast through strange lands with strange people, strange lands controlled by strange people, it did not feel safe, and train slowed down. Mosquitoes followed the freight cars and swarmed inside the boxes and just outside the doors, but bear was accustomed to mosquito getting at them and didn't mind at all. Theocean did and couldn't imagine how he'd sleep in this car, this night, with all the bugs, and stay cool too. He was more than a little concerned. *I will be more content when we get through and clear of this place.*

He took a pill and opened a bottle of wine. He was tired of spending time on this train. Oh, the ride had been beautiful but seeing so much economic depression had made him sad. Why, just north of here, a skinny woman had hailed the train. She was not far from a lake that once cupped water but now was an empty bowl, and the people there were starving. Somehow its libraries were still open and they had news of life from a larger world and the hungry woman with so little hope was familiar with the survivor movement, and all those living Another Way, and wanted to get to a parkland, and fast.

Here had been blights and several freezes, she said, that wiped out most of the larger family farms and only a few remained. At two of the lake's beach heads people were still trading for what few commodities were available for day to day living. There was one crummy junk store there and an even crummier pawn shop associated with a denomination Theocean was not familiar with. Another woman was there with the woman who flagged the train, along with her son. They sold fruit from the back of a pickup that no longer ran—their orchards still yielded—and they wanted out too.

They can thank Agod for their good sense, he thought.

Theocean was sitting at the edge of a car – its doors flung open. His legs dangled while he took in the wide open view recording like a film in his mind while the train dragged along. It was too hot to sleep. The air smelled sweetly still, like sea grapes and salt, and he heard all kinds of macerations below him, all kinds of critters on the ground crunching, chewing, spitting out organic stuff. Worms were eating trees alive and he was thinking he wouldn't want to tent camp here; too many bugs and critters in the earth, his tent floor didn't tightly zip and there was so much decomposing matter on the ground it made him squirmish. He did like the way the vultures looked hunched in silhouette against the night sky, they reminded him of early cartoons he had watched in his youth. He shined his light on the earth floor to see what was doing all the chewing and making those loud, clanking noises.

The dumpsters aren't locked so there is no bear here, he thought. *What the heck can that be? I'll be damned . . .* and scratching his head he turned off the light. It was attracting too many bugs.

An owl flew by the open door. *I wonder what's being discussed in those campgrounds he thought. I wonder . . .*

Those camps were survivors' camps and signs everywhere were of people reacting against the rise of technology and binary code. Instead they celebrated life as human beings, not robots. Fake money, in a make-believe world of binary code central bankers and corporatists had pushed upon them, had brought serfdom and life-time servitude to banks, but life as it existed in a society before technology and mock, now, that's where it was at.

Oh, Agod, give me strength to endure this train ride, thought Theocean. *Oh, it's for the bears, I know, but this place is not my home, I'm just passing through. I'll be glad when we reach Antarctica.*

Taking that pill and drinking the bottle of wine and stuck on the train allowed Theocean some moments with his inner self he might not have had otherwise. He more than sighed . . . sighed deeply, down deeply. America had been a violent nation and there were not many people left there now . . . it was no longer a big attraction. Theocean was thinking the way a man thinks who had sympathies with strong anti-corporatist, anti-central banker critiques of the contemporary world order. He knew about struggle and a hard life and assessed the value and usefulness of survivors by determining if they could plant a garden, thatch a roof, split wood . . . pray and practice reverence. He laughed heartily, down deeply, deep down inside.

Survivors were up early. The birds had come through and cleaned out the scraps and crumbs from the evening meals. Blackbirds and doves flew together from one campsite to the next and a young red-shouldered hawk screeched from a nearby branch. Hawk was the first thing everyone in the campground heard in the morning and later again in the afternoon. Hawk came within feet of every camper in the campground. It was tame and hunted salamanders, geckos, and newts out from under their feet.

The campers were from all over, to the left from Alaska, east of here from Michigan, and still others from Ontario . . . damn cold there. The young hawks were raised by these campers. A few of them, men and women, boys and girls, entire families, were dressed in jungle camouflaged shirts, trousers and boots. A sportsman camped closer to the canals and painted everything he saw around him, on the road and in the campgrounds, around every corner, like Highway Men did all those years ago. After noon they all scavenged for wood and took fishing rods and, casting nets along the canals, searched for their suppers.

Live oak stood, dead, rotting north-northwest on a downward slope, falling away from the animated campground. The rail wound its way from the tents and stoves into another area. Winds were high and increasing in strength with the morning's sunshine, accelerating into blustery, gusty gales in the afternoon, and with cooler temperatures than previous days, it was not a prevailing weather pattern. Theocean watched the wind change shape and metamorphose into a rainy, stormy night. *Live oak will heat their hearths during the evening's storm,* he thought.

Some had adapted to new habitats and temperature change. Those who could moved around, and in strange climates and terrains, learned to eat differently, changed their diets and managed, somehow, in new environments. Others couldn't and became extinct. Gopher turtle couldn't adapt, certainly was not adaptable, and didn't leave the hammock. Oh, some tried but when crossing the streets, people in automobiles, at three dollars a gallon, crushed and flattened them into the pavement in pursuit of fast food and recreation because, for some ungodly reason, fast food was more important than a gopher turtle's life.

Theocean couldn't fathom this. It was such sin and Agod was angry with humankind and in the end Earth tilted violently in disapproval and reacted harshly to an electromagnetic field jammed with the movement of binary code and mock, shaking loose a solar explosion that fried all of technology's circuits. Afterwards, for a long, long while, people killed and ate each other and when the earth's population was finally under control, survivors began to live Another Way.

Clipena and her pelicans assumed air support at the border. Canada's geese turned round and flew home, and pelican accompanied bear to the isthmus.

It was almost midnight and the bears heard crickets. It rained all day and the moon was full now, the breeze and dark night had cooled down the land. The wind changed from the southwest to the northeast. Last night the wind lay down and it was hot, but not tonight. This evening it was cool and windy and breezy, switching from the south to the north.

Theocean was still on the train and tonight as it chugged along, he was not seeing what he saw but was entranced. The sight of a green pond lulled him towards involuntary thoughts and he was stimulated further, mindlessly illuminated.

The green light in the pool spoke and presented dappled moonlight, awakened full from rains in a hidden hammock pond. Vibrating light colored pool green, reflecting all colors of light, visible and invisible. There was a place on this spectrum, a liminal place, where if one placed himself there, one could see invisible light, if one looked hard enough, and hear its message, and Theocean knew this.

Birds sang in the moonlight in this earthly paradise and invisible color and light enchanted. Flora and fauna had invisible color and made inaudible sound and while photosynthesis made its circuit round dense jungle parks in daylight, floral and fauna absorbed the power of invisible light, and its intelligence.

A woman with long blond hair, kind of wavy, wearing a phosphorescent robe was circling the green pool that night. She was on a bicycle, a red one, and dressed like a prophet. The bears and Theocean watched her from the train, and she appeared to be just looking around and taking in the sights. She took good care of herself and was maybe, oh, twenty years old.

She hopped off her bicycle and in her phosphorescent robe, picked a stick from off the ground and stirred the surface of the pool, parting its living algae. The woman had abandoned technology. Whether one was young or old, beautiful or ugly and healthy or not one could appreciate life and the earth and its gift if one abandoned tracking devices, and technology. It was the only way now – the woman with long blond hair knew it and she was looking for a sign.

Walking the path of his life, Theocean saw a lot of men and women holding tightly to their tech devices, looking burnt-out. This young woman was healthy looking, she took good care of herself and it occurred to those who saw her she was just passing through – but in fact this place was her home.

She was, indeed, living Another Way, and managing very well, very well indeed. She survived and cast her net wide. When one abandoned technology one survived, it was as simple as that. She cast her net on land and over water; there were many ways, more than most were aware of, to cast a net and live well.

Bankers, over time, had created an economy, a global economy that roped people into working like serfs and, making mock for them and their rich corporatist friends tossed the serfs left-over crumbs. This became more important than living a good life on the planet and while as good as suicide, many took the poison bait because they didn't understand, they didn't understand how bankers had been encumbering peoples' past, present and future, shackling them with debt, teasing them always with more and more, always more, while all the time Earth presented people with everything they needed, and mortgaging their prosperity, caught most in leg traps, paralyzing them with greed and debt.

It had been too easy to lead people around by the nose, way too easy. Why, once technology was applied to every damn aspect of life, people nearly completely destroyed Earth, and at an utterly fast pace while on the way to fast food. Why were so many in a rush to consume the whole planet? Eat fast, get the most, was that it? What did bankers and elites want? To control the whole world and all its assets then leave for Mars when living became untenable on Earth? Or to render people redundant, perhaps obsolete? *Are you kidding me?* What attributes of humankind had bankers and corporatist tapped into that allowed them, almost, to rule the whole world and destroy the planet? *Oh, what a close call and what needed to change?*

To begin with, abandon technology.

The wind tickled the needles on the pines and they danced above the pool against a gray night. There was suddenly a lot of cloud action high up in the sky and the needles were feeling it, feeling the wind, way down low. The bears fell asleep and Theocean flew towards the pool.

The story the beautiful young woman with the long blond hair told Theocean and anyone for that matter, anyone anywhere in the world where birds flew overhead, geese, gulls, hawks, ibis, egrets, heron, and ducks over any earthly garden she happened to pass through, was that we live in a world that ought to be treated like the paradise it is.

I work in a garden eight months a year, Theocean. Then cold, frozen ice covers the garden and I get up on my bicycle and travel the world.

Intelligence wants to communicate with intelligence so let's not quibble about that. People simply must stop listening to and reading media reports and learn to think for themselves, and trust Agod. They simply can't afford another day of being led around by the noses.

Do you know what a crane in Asia told me? It said it watched while some in Asia buried land mines and blew up their own kind. What idiots. We don't want that here, do we?

The elites, today's aristocrats, have very easily, too easily, with the help of mock and technology, controlled people and led them around by the noses for too long now, and it must end.

Birds everywhere watched as larger−than−life heavy equipment moved the earth around and sucked out fossil fuels from the bowels of the earth, substances that should have remained in the bowels of the earth. How greedy and stupid, and in a world of dwindling resources and exponentially expanding population growth? C'mon now!

What almost happened here in the Occident, what almost happened is the whole, hot, tired, old world came here and began to buy everything out from under us, with our mock. Can you believe it? Somehow, someway the whole world had a lot of the West's currency, more than the West did, in fact, and they had their eyes on the state and federal parklands, the jewels in our crowns, and everything else. Yes, the whole world swarmed here, to the two continents, but Earth tilted and threw their electromagnetic fields into disarray and spoiled the bankers' plan and now the whole occidental world is bunched up in refugee camps and parklands and though some still handle their affairs with mock, most simply barter and trade. South of the isthmus there is a refugee

camp section ten times the size of most and a big congregation of dusk people sits there.
You must speak with them Theocean.

And with that she got back up on her red bicycle and rode away.

A mockingbird was perched on a branch in a small tree along the edge of a campsite where the dusk people sat. It was late in the afternoon and mockingbird was not particularly doing anything but simply placed on the wind, casually turning its head one way then another, not feeding or singing, but resting and relaxed and looking one way then another, its shiny little eyes gleamed while oily black shimmered off its beak in the sunlight.

Serial numbers on the mock identified those for whom the mock had been issued, someone was saying.

A big congregation of dusk people sat together, in chairs. Dusk people, a large group of them, were sitting together, struggling, trying to find words to explain to the youngsters amongst them what had happened in America. They were getting wet, sitting there they got all wet and although it was not raining, the wind whipped moisture into froths and draped it over the people while they sat in the dusk.

Dusk with color was extraordinary and the color of sky at dusk beyond dusk people was not particularly brilliant blue, no, not brilliant blue but baby blue, and behind that rose orange, an orange rose, not brilliant yet, baby still, and tinted the blue gray, with yellow and orange and white.

The absurdity of bankers extended so far that when Agod decided white bear must be moved to Antarctica, Theocean and Geela got on board for the long, slow ride, and oh my Agod, what bankers didn't do on the table, they did under it and all along the route the whole off-the-books economy was in plain sight – the view from the train was extraordinary really, larger than life.

After the pill and bottle of wine the twirling, swirling, whirly piece of Theocean's mind, the part that curled where thoughts went round and round, just before that place epiphany occurred. Funny thing was he had perked up and, looking one way then another for a sign, it had fallen in his lap. He took hold of it and carried it around for awhile and when it dropped white light extinguished, went out and he wasn't twirling or swirling or whirling any longer, he wasn't in the circle any more. A linear distinction emerged and a time and place where one decides if one will help out or not, if one cares or not, if one loves or not was presented to him. This was where Theocean was, way out in front, on holy ground, at a crossroads, waiting for the others to catch up.

Even though binary code had exploded in the electromagnetic fields a few bankers were left and exchanged mock for things in tight, vestigial, aristocratic worlds and, because it was still needed, the laundry machine on the isthmus continued to operate.

There had been problems with the supply of mock; it had expanded too fast and all the cash was not returned to central bankers as arranged but found its way into the hands of those who would try and almost succeed in buying the whole country out from under us.

The local economy on the isthmus was a mock one . . . cocaine purchases certainly were not put on credit cards so cash was everywhere – a lot of it. These purchases were accounted for in the world of bankers and governments in a manner different from binary code and, unaccountably, all mock was counted and piled high, in depots and storage facilities and an off-the-books accounting system swelled all over the world.

But why cocaine?

Oh, it was a great launderer, a great whitener, a great laundry detergent. It got all the stains out. The isthmus was a great place to do laundry, its shape like that of a big washing machine, the old-fashioned kind with the ringer on top and with a dose, with a shot in the arm and a boost from this laundry agent, like magic, the money supply increased and effects of earlier laundry treatments were renewed, wiping clean all traces of stain and everywhere along the canal, after a wash, dirty laundry, now clean, was strung out to dry, all along the canal.

Theocean burped. He had heard well the dusk people and their conversations and wanted to shake things up and make things happen, get up on another rail, a rail shooting through the electromagnetic fields. It was a spiritual quest, his country needed him, he needed himself, but there wasn't much room for his power to work in the atmosphere . . . bankers had jammed the airwaves with binary code.

I get the hiccups when I drink too much, thought Theocean. *I've noticed that in the past. He laughed. But there are very important things I think of when I let my hair down a bit and it's not so bad, except for the hiccups, and the headaches. Oh, I need a night that lasts about, oh, I don't know, twenty or thirty years, maybe longer.*

He was tired. Theocean's power exhausted him and he was very tired.

Chapter 28

A pack of hounds gave chase. They worked hard to take out the weak performers and polar bears' prospects didn't look good.

Outside squalls of peepers and wood frogs trilled crescendo then dropped silence. Their rhythm lulled bear and train rolled along on the track. Broadening then sustained peeper sounds and frog cacophonies rang in an acoustically hypnotic trance from outside the train, and wandered towards bear, where they sat on pools of ice, keeping cool. Bulls croaked and bullied percussion and bear fell asleep. Their sounds hung in a liminal place now and, humming soliloquy, spoke-talked, as bears fell asleep. Bear was beginning to understand, or so bear thought. Between dreamtime and consciousness bull frogs' chimes floated then suspended and bear understood. Even the little peeps, oh my Agod, were they ever enthusiastic about waking up from that long winter, and its deep, cold freeze.

The bulls bellowed. Bear altered perspective and changed worlds. Drugs were not needed. Bear knew how to travel down and journey through the noise to the place where inarticulate language shaped sound into audible blocks and bear understood.

The reprobates, Papel, Stoonman, and Tossherrheim tracked Geela and following like bloodhounds, did their best to stop her. They didn't want white bear to reach Antarctica or the Wilderness League to succeed in anything it attempted, particularly if the League was cooperating with survivors living Another Way, the parkland way. It would simply embolden too many and encourage their power and influence.

Agod has been good to me, Theocean thought. *And this has been a good trip. Thank you, Agod.* The wind was blowing and he was living out of doors; almost sixty years old and living outside of doors . . . and still alive. His power had revealed itself to him several times on this trip, and he was grateful.

Then there was Geela, Agod's daughter, the superstar from America's origin myth, thought Theocean.

Geela was propelled and targeted objects larger than she was and conquered and prevailed.

But she had forgotten how powerful she was. Then one day memories flooded her mind and she recalled the many feats that had awed the witnesses to her life, unselfish acts, most of which had never been recorded, yet many had sung her praises. Geela endured and strength and courage flowed through her veins again, and with a purpose larger than she had ever imagined.

Agod was revealed through conversations with the Wilderness League. Agod was both mother and father and Agod's daughter Geela was the mask representing intelligence, and accord. She had seen both sides and imparted an understanding, unmasked the duality of the American myth that, if allowed to continue, would extend the waiver for greedy corporatists to play people and continue to make slaves out of them and, in the process, completely and utterly ruin the country, its land and people, their culture and wilderness too.

After her time at Treasury and, remember, Geela had been conscripted . . . she chose Another Way and spent the rest of her life encouraging people to live in accord with nature, and to be grateful. In other words, quit the game while you're ahead, refuse to play or participate, you are the pawns without whom these rich corporatists cannot play. She got it; only the animals could save humans and earth from destruction. House Boat People understood too. Tribes huddled around fracking sites didn't get it but some Cold People were rethinking . . .

Some campground dwellers were enlightened while others were not, and tension and conflict continued to exist. People who dwelled in new New York City, the American aristocracy, central bankers, those in Washington, Treasury, corporatists and globalists—they were all intelligent, sure enough—were afraid of losing power, and mock and wealth, and resisted any effort to live Another Way, and continued to impose duality upon the people.

Agod was angry and issued an ultimatum. *Live Another Way, the parkland way. Get rid of fake money . . . or else.*

Flamingo flew overhead, screeching, their pink a sign of hope for Geela. She was being tested again and with her this year's winter near its end, another spring of hers was waiting to be born. *Have you ever seen a starling-sized bird scatter a flock of jays?*

So this little man, Tossherrheim . . . he's really a little piece of crap in the scheme of things, isn't he . . . with his binary code, and all. He's a piece of cake . . . a piece of little-crap cake . . . Don't forget, Geela, corporatists and governments can't do what they do without the survivors . . . Tossherrheim will not last . . . he too will pass.

An ambush was planned and carefully executed at a place where the track was blocked for market day, and it was a big day. Peddlers, men and women and children, were selling things, anything, all things from within: drugs, gold, jewelry, stones, land, deeds, bonds, body parts, bodies and any item at all that had been previously stuffed in safe deposit boxes around the world. Now these safe things belonged to everyone, and no one. Men and women hawked rich peoples' stuff. Across the street self-serve car washes and abandoned chevrons and circles were replaced with laundromats; economically ruined properties bordered the perimeter. It was a depressing place but anything one wanted could be found at this market whether it was useful or not. This was the heart of the hemisphere's cash district, a former international transportation hub, surrounded by jungle and agricultural districts, and all kinds of stuff could be got under the shadows of the few, remaining, well-maintained municipal buildings; binary code didn't interfere with the distribution of wealth here.

The train carrying bear rammed into the marketplace and jumped track, causing all the cash to scatter into the fog while bear fell into the too warm sea. An emergency ensued. Geela needed help, and fast. She was just southeast of Tossherrheim's position and requested reinforcements and all the assistance she could get.

Jumping Beans quickly arrived and worked hard to save the bears. Greet sent her Jumping Beans in to pull the soaking wet and too warm bears from the tepid water, quickly now, before they all perished and died from the heat. Jumping Beans were always willing to help, and didn't need to be told.

Papel slipped in and tied a rope around Tomon's neck, and Cort's too. Tomon Carr and Cort Orman were on the train and good company for bear but along the edge of the canal Papel forced them to take alcohol and drugs and dive deep for the cold-water bears that had slipped from inside the comfort of the train into the too warm water.

Kill the bears and grab all the money. Bring it back to me, Tossherrheim told them. *Tie ropes around their necks . . . and choke them . . . if those cormorants try and swallow any money.*

The old growth sequoias came to Geela's aid and Greylock's old growth forest, a small group of spruce that had walked all the way from the East Coast to accompany the bears and Geela in solidarity helped too. Sequoia hoisted and Greylock lifted and together they worked and saved the bears. Sequoia and Greylock represented the future of the planet and its survival to so many in the Wilderness League and they had had enough strength and courage and plant intelligence to lift and right the heavy rail cars. Tossherrheim hadn't counted on their help.

Papel and Stoonman, Tossherrheim and other villains tried to control the good cormorants, but they turned and dove deep, dragging Papel and Stoonman with them once the drugs they took wore off. Somehow Tossherrheim managed to stay dry, but again his usual mock didn't materialize. *What's up with that?*

Tossherrheim was angry and would have killed them all but so many from the Wilderness League were helping and together got bear in the cars, one at a time, back on track. Tossherrheim was out-numbered. House Boat dwellers had arrived and turtles from the Sargasso Sea, Fig Sherkin and Erhon Geren, Pilson Bloo and Caren Shilland. Everyone in the Wilderness League came and helped bear.

Like Cold People, Stoonman finally woke and opened his eyes. His mind clicked on and, yes, he was scared, but no more fight, no struggle with layers of dense fog or stifling heat and shape shifting stabs of pain from drugs and alcohol. No, he was not doing that no more; he was switching sides, and soon. He no longer wanted to be part of Tossherrheim's plan, and certainly didn't want to kill polar bears so Stoonman abandoned technology and jumped on the caravan on its way to the South Pole.

So, from here, next day, who ran and which way?

Leaving the isthmus Theocean wondered what the bugs would be like in South America. He had never been to South America though Theocean had heard the land was beautiful. Would there be enough water along the way?

They passed through the isthmus and began the southern leg of the journey that had begun when Agod gave the order to move the bears. Stoonman was with them now and the caravan was travelling to the South Pole by way of the Inka Highway. *The Inka Highway? The great Inka road, the same 45,000 mile interstate stretch that united all kinds of people and took forty years and all those billions to construct that had, five hundred years earlier, been built mostly without benefit of iron or wheel? And people think we can't move bear? Are you kidding me?*

Good night Geela. I feel love from everyone in the Wilderness League. We have been fortunate to make this trip, and using trees' plant intelligence, the caravan continued to wind its way to the South Pole. They stopped at camps along the way, South American survivor camps, parklands and federal lands. That was the plan anyway. Those on the train certainly didn't want to ride all day and night and miss the people along the way. Well, maybe just that last leg. Bear wouldn't mind because bear was going home. *No, bear won't mind and neither will I,* thought Theocean, *because I am going home too.*

The fireflies, the ones that had not been tracked or traced or captured by sovereign nations, those flies managed a hack into central banks and using optical code revealed to the world an audit of sorts, and shining the light, changed everything, and those who could think for themselves understood and those who couldn't, finally, reluctantly began to understand, whether they liked it or not.

Corporate economies were larger than nations. Bankers printed mock for corporations and globalists, not for the people, but distributed to them only crumbs. The world was no longer a world of sovereign nations but one of corporations and globalists. They tried hard to take control of the whole world using mock and killed the gold standard, switching it off during a depression. Later, deep in the woods, while the Wilderness League and fireflies listened, bankers and corporatists conspired to create a bipolar life in America, one of mania and depression, manic then depressed, and hoarding all gold, bankers buried it deep in vaults and, forcing people to use mock and value their assets in terms of fiat money, outlawed gold as a popular currency, eroding real value.

Enough of that, thought Theocean. *Thank Agod we had the fireflies.*

Later, after bear was safely back on the train, on their way to Antarctica, Greet Withe stood alone near a pond, watching grebes sail and float about, surrounded by a road that cars, once upon a time drove round and round on and, tightly turning the corners, circled closer, round and round, all going in the same direction, all driving one way. The grebes sailed and floated, drifting occasionally . . . aloft. With a flutter, wind power tacked and grebe, with a little paddle, realigned its steering. The pond's surface was silvery and white where wind whipped up its surface, but otherwise the color of pond was deep and still, without much benefit of light.

Standing in utter awe and amazement, Greet Withe doffed her plumage, her plumed crown, and in deference to grebe's superior ability and power took off her fancy gloves, and bowed.

Chapter 29

Sunday's sun went down and twilight approached. A festival was winding down in a nearby campground and music roamed around just outside the train, playing a few last notes of sunshine jazz and bird warmth. It didn't get any better.

While on the road the caravan travelers met all kinds of people and heard their stories, and music soothed and adjusted their points of view. Geela had missed it, it felt right, like an adventure ought to, like life ought to feel around those who were idly wild.

Next day the train drove through cultivated fields just north of somewhere south of them. Each mile the plants were a little higher, the furrows a little greener; brown and green stretched and yawned in the sun and swarmed the earth and brown earth turned green overnight, linear green spirits sprouted rows, and the spirit of green, everyday magic, shot up from the earth.

It was cooler now. The wind was blowing hard from the northwest and train was ascending. Theocean was in his compartment warming up with coffee and a small heater. Ice came and stayed on the cars, ice on the windows, and in the morning in the saucepans.

Coming along the edge of a ridge, a plateau stretched beneath them into the horizon and looking down into it he saw hundreds and hundreds and thousands and thousands of survivors tent camping like native tribes did once upon a time, North and South Americans, doing it just to do it, idly wild.

Oh, I don't know, sighed Theocean. *Why did government give away the land to the whole world? Ought not they have returned the land and wilderness to its first people, and survivors, and not give it away to the whole world? Other people were other countries' concerns, were they not? This land did not belong to the whole world or the corporatists or bankers either . . .*

Birds were curious and flew alongside survivors, listening to the sounds of their voices, and the songs they sang. They watched as survivors expressed themselves and liked the way they smelled. Maybe they liked the way they looked too.

Geela was for the birds, and she knew it. Birds watched people as much and probably more often than people watched birds. They had to, in order to survive, and besides, they harbinged things to come, it was their nature.

On the trail heading south towards Antarctica, four deer stood still in the great wide open, in front of a shrub, and watched the train approach; deer ducked behind the shrub and fled once the train was out of sight. In the sky above, the big sky, the flat-bottomed clouds stood still and the clouds above the flat-bottomed clouds, the ones with gray and blue in them, were in motion, but the flat-bottomed clouds stood in one place over the landscape, some saturated with light, others with moisture. Then sky turned storm black and ominous, and up ahead, the rain came.

The clouds in motion had faces in them, partially hidden faces of early North and South American superheroes long gone, rubbed out, killed years ago. Resurrecting them was painful and embarrassing . . . shameful and didn't fit the hemisphere's contemporary, adoptive narrative, but they were there, nonetheless, great-grandmothers and great-grandfathers and powerful and mighty animals, if one looked hard enough, like Cotteeman did, for instance.

Thick flocks of jays moved from tree to tree, darting rays of blue light. They flew from out of the shadows and circled the superheroes. It was just blue and gray then only blue, then more blue than gray, no white or light at all. Still vibrant, yes, but without the light blue and gray dissolved in distant showers and watercolors streaked and washed above the green and gold and brown and red terrains.

On the land below people recreated. There was lots of enjoyment here among outdoor people, recreationalists and sportsmen, where blue and gray rained. Their lives were in motion and they wouldn't have it any other way; not postured and posed, looking out over a view, but in motion, people living their lives in motion. Jay frequented these places and heralded the arrivals and departures of survivors in the blue and the gray, trying to show them the way.

Wind was artist here. Wind painted gray and on the canvas gray swirled from off the palette and the white, well, white was light, and the wind painted over all of this, in the air on an electromagnetic canvas, which many didn't see. It was jammed now with too much binary code.

There were big gaps in the white clouds, and behind them it was gray: heavy gray, leaden gray, black-duck gray. The flat-bottomed clouds were way over there now and, less threatening, over towards the north and somewhat towards the south, the remaining westerly positioned clouds had lost their storminess and motion and looked like a bunch of soggy, wet cotton balls; sagging, soaked batten balls stuffed in a bag and without their shape, watercolor dripped. Brush stroked and dubbed blue on the clouds and, under the dubbing, gray saturated blue and, muddying the water, shifted the air. It was cooler now, and the drafts, pulling one way and then another, crept in from one place or another and across Theocean's skin, shadowing the rain.

There was fluidity on the road, and here in the campgrounds and in peoples' lives. Their paths crossed from time to time and they shared notes and experiences under the blue and the gray, and then continued along on the paths of their lives. Lives in motion, here then gone, and the caravan passed through one place just as soon as it left another.

Americans viewed themselves in well-framed myths while government worked its people real good: screaming media, earphones, the sounds of horror and madness. How does one transcend and not break, and another attach to the sound and the fury, get carried off and lost forever in the public address and then, perhaps, after the noise drops off, somewhere, a person stops thinking and NEVER retrieves ones' former self?

Attaching oneself to the fury, the noise and the voices was dangerous. *Do we want this to happen to ourselves?*

Soon the whole country was camping out, waiting for that heart attack on the road. Government failed its people but made the corporatists rich, super rich beyond their wildest imaginations.

Then anhinga flew in front of it all wearing a brown cape. Some anhingas wore capes when they went out and others did not and this one reminded all who saw it they were not dressed for the occasion.

Chapter 30

Occo and Lithil listened to the magic book until the story was over. They liked it enough to tell all their friends and in this way the tale spread over the land.

Bald cypress stood against a gray and blue sky and the trees looked extraordinary. Bear wasn't accustomed to seeing those colors and shapes together and didn't know what to make of them. Another landscape . . . or perhaps a moonscape? No, they decided the trees were all their relatives, skeletal aspects of dead relatives, monuments erected to those long gone, waiting to be kissed goodbye.

Rolling through the bald and the dwarves, the trees washed gray and white and naked and stood against a sky opposing the sun. Sky was gray, but not true. Was it smudged from an emerging smog and dry with no moisture? Or fouled from a grass fire?

Then the fields lit up. Orange was there, inside the gray, and the train drove through the burning fields where fire caught and black smoke billowed. Smoke reached the clouds and clouds turned orange, reflecting the flames, then water separated color and some of it rolled back, rolled back down into the inferno.

It was fantastic. Orange soared into the clouds, smoke curled upwards, twirling, swirling upwards ahead of orange towards a flat-bottomed sky, gray flat-bottomed sky, and was trapped. There orange turned pink and was set free, and it was all so divine.

The pink as it passed was revealed to those bears with a polarized lens, without it, well, it was not possible to see and the rose tinted clouds, the coral and the rose, were missed. Bear laughed nervously, trembled with laughter, and sucked in their breath. Bear hadn't expected this, just here, and so far along on their journey. They choked on quick, short sobs and so despondent and disappointed in human beings, they cried out, *Please Agod we are struggling and afraid.* But whatever it was they were witnessing just outside the train was powerful and encouraging enough to give them hope. They just had to get through it all and get back home, back home on the ice.

A short distance from the ground, sky turned suddenly blue just above scorched cypress standing tall like gravestones and sky through naked color and trees with no foliage looked after life and, as still as a cemetery along this stretch, out of the graveyard into the light, life emerged, surreally so, and bear liked it. There was no green, still no green along this stretch. Then train arched wide past a bend and the landscape leaned into green, and bear changed worlds.

A little after nightfall Theocean looked out over the firmament through an open door. He was living outside and he liked it. He really liked it and had arranged his bed on the rail so he could look out through the open door while he reposed. Tonight his bed faced the short shrubby brush outside and he could see the sky and the stars from where he lay and though it was not a view of great, big, open sky but peeks of sky, and it was glorious. Out over the shrub just outside the train, behind them, was a cluster of trees with long pine needles and the trees with the long pine needles grew tall and thin, and at the top, high above their trunks was the shape of a dog, a dog down on all fours . . . kneeling . . . and dog was praying. Theocean couldn't get over it and the dog, because sky had a light, filmy cloud cover dimming its stars that evening, was easy to spot in silhouette and meant more to him than the funeral pyre or any other sign shown to him along the way.

In another car the young men and women among them had promised to be quiet but they were drinking. They were drinking and they had promised they wouldn't. But they were, and they had those big bottles, the big, two-liter ones, filled with bourbon.

They were good youngsters from good families. They spoke well, and were polite and Theocean listened as they murmured in the darkness. They had high hopes for their futures and talked like young people do when first tasting an ardent spirit. As the evening advanced their conversations wandered, but the particulars weren't important. Theocean couldn't hear the details, nor did he want to. He was listening to the collective voice as it emerged and developed its own rhythm in response to the voice of the group's leader and its melody and two-part harmony filled Theocean's mind.

As the night advanced and the authoritative voice of the leader told story, the group responded, singing loud and clearly:

WHOAwoawoawoaWHOAWHOAWHOA YES or

WHOAwoawoawoaWHOAWHOAWHOA NO and in

this way the collective joined in and, by way of refrain, built a bridge. The children of survivors acknowledged or rejected story's truth, and were instrumental in sustaining its myth, or not, around firelight and bourbon.

Occo said, "The important thing Lithil is that survivors can think for themselves now. They stopped listening to media. If the remainers don't do the same and abandon technology and live the parkland way they will be tracked and hunted and cornered just like the wild animals and all the first people were, on behalf of the corporatists and bankers, until safely subdued, or dead."

"The state and federal palatinates and their proprietors, corporations and banks and the signatories of world trade agreements, had the prerogatives of the super rich in mind and wanted to control the whole world."

Geela had her home in an aerie. She was Agod's daughter, but somehow Tossherrheim had managed a climb up the steep rocks and got inside her nest. Over the years and one fight after another, Geela had taken several swipes at Tossherrheim. She wanted to knock him out of her nest, wanted to fling him over the cliffs and watch him plunge to his death. She wanted him out, out of her country, once and for all. This was her country, after all and Geela took on the Treasury, bankers, rich trading partners, and those that provided cheap money and cheap labor, corporatists, and everyone else who wreaked havoc on the country, the world, and the environment too, heck, the whole gang.

"Why adopt technology in a time of dwindling resources and an exponentially expanding world population? Are you idiots? People want purpose, a life . . . not to be rendered irrelevant," insisted Geela.

She searched high and low and long and hard for intelligence and found so very little of it, actually, very few signs of it, unless of course she was among survivors in the parklands, and Tossherrheim, oh, Tossherrheim, with his posture of verisimilitude, and its redolence, faintly evocative of superpower's soft power of imposing oppressive regimes without anyone really noticing, stunk here in her nest.

"Geela's idea of success was to run the corporate aristocracy off and out of the land, make stuffed straw dolls of them and place them in museums, museums that reminded people of what they had almost become," Theocean mused.

"She didn't trust any arrangement that involved compromise, and wanted to knock them out, out of her nest once and for all. All people who had decided to live like greedy, over-consuming fat ducks and not respect the life of a gopher turtle had no value in her world anymore— the time for forbearance was over."

"Political correctness, what's that? A crap phrase, an affectation . . . really . . . a form of censorship."

Independent thoughts and the ability to produce them had atrophied. Constant bombardment from television, radio, phones and other devices disguised the actual context of content, avoiding any real understanding with a super text of white, distracting noise, and this was very dangerous. Media had used their medium to control opinions and make mock and, oh, so much had been at stake. Like binary code, the sum of one for them and zero for you was counted so far into negative territory by powerful, greedy manipulators, that it soon became unmanageable, and incomprehensible to most.

Government had mortgaged the country's prosperity and posterity. It shorted any wealth people ever managed to accumulate and arbitraged their standard of living. This was their inheritance and the Wilderness League didn't like it, didn't like it at all, not one bit.

My power exhausts me, Theocean thought.

Technology's reptilian shadow lengthened. Its mass shifted and drifted one day covering the whole land while most (mammals) were eating and eating some more. Under its total and consummate reach, stomachs filled and bloated beyond capacity. People couldn't move and were trapped.

A lull fell. Everywhere cars were parked and not in motion and the few survivors on the road had it all to themselves. Then wind bellowed and the breadth of Agod screamed out. The laws of nature had not been well understood and so many hadn't listened . . . hadn't wanted to hear.

When wind lied down the breadth of Agod was something to be inferred. The Wilderness League understood this, and the survivors too but many others were deaf. So wind percussed and tickled leaves and wind sounded like running water, and tinkling noise was leaves rustling. But gentleness was not enough so branches swayed and trunks creaked and heaving wildly, trees were tossed about and shaken from their roots on upward, as human beings will be tossed one day.

People were not feeling well; they lay down and like reptiles didn't move because, heck, if they did they'd blow up. But people couldn't help themselves and hoisted for more so nature's vengeance came and those mammals who ate way too much and somnambulated like reptiles perished. But those in the parklands, the ones who had hit the road, survived and had it all to themselves.

This very wind, the breadth of Agod, buffeted crow, and while crow played with glittering objects and rolled balls and slid in the snow and flew over survivors who moved across the same terrain as fox, they listened. The breadth of Agod was filtered through trees and talkative leaves delivered the message, the one explaining everyday way, to any who cared to listen, and live well.

Chapter 31

The seeds for growing food were tossed and found again. In fact most things survivors needed could be found strewn in compost heaps and garbage dumps all over the land. The Happy People in Sequoia knew this and chose to live in trees and let plant intelligence show them the way.

For a while many survivors drifted with turtle on the Sargasso Sea and, clinging to seaweed, floated along on calm waters, trying to forget about it all. But in curved recesses along the coastline large, colorful blooms draped over all the other growth and in a welcoming gesture, encouraged those indifferent ones to return home.

The vine-like plants had points on the edges of their blooms and unassumingly their satin spines followed a raised ridge over webs of petal and past their many obvolutions reached the points, the tips on the stars encircled in a fabric of web. At times these stars opened flat like a discus, but in other moments appeared trumpet-like and blew horns and made music, deep, blue, yellow-sunshine jazz. It was marvelous, and beckoned those floating with turtle. When vibration of bright sunlight washed away color for a minute, musical syllables mirrored the lyrical ones invading the minds of those drifting with turtle and they floated and bobbed in an image reflected off the sea, a reflection in a dream image, and when skies colored again those drifting with turtle were greeted by morning's glory and rising sun, and people let go and waded towards the shore, and turtle laid eggs again along the coast.

Geela and company were almost in Antarctica. Polar bears were dreaming of arctic char and Geela was dreaming she was flying with Agod and Greet Withe. She thought about the magic book she had held onto so tightly for so many years and lost. But the old woman had picked it up and was sharing the story with everyone she knew. *Good . . . it is time . . . I need help.*

Theocean was an apparition. He wore a shadow skirt and slipped between mortal life and death and soul immortality. He was Cotteeman, and invisible. He had been invited . . . no . . . not asked, but taken by the hand and spirited to the place where arrival departed and departure arrived, the place where the dead go to be kissed goodbye. Where one age ends and a new one begins.

Today prairie dogs were smiling and dousing for clean, clear, potable water. But just yesterday they had dropped and disappeared. Who knows? Tomorrow they may march again across *la prairie* and, with all its native plants and humming insect life, take over, and perhaps the Cold People will stay on and live Another Way.

Bear made it to the South Pole and penguin was glad for their company. They taught bear to hunt penguin way so bear wouldn't think of them as number one food source.

It's possible that very soon the Wilderness League will turn bankers' perspectives and conceptions of the world inside out. No longer will it be fashionable to take it all and bill it to mock exchanges, to ordinary people, and kill and sanction anyone who stands in the way. It will no longer be possible, because it will be all gone.

And though their numbers will be greatly diminished, some will manage to survive and live on earth as true partners with the animals and birds. They will thrive and despite the former greed and avarice of the corporate class, the world will begin to mend and heal. There was hope.

Frost bit diamonds into the rain. Survivors joined hands and circled the earth and binding their grateful selves towards heaven they reached for the sky and gave thanks and praise to Agod. Love for the earth emerged. True love spread out and enveloped the world.

And the people from the Circle, the brave ones who accompanied bear to the South Pole stood on their heads, upside down, rather than on their feet right side up, and laughed and giggled. In their pleasure the brave ones looked upon the world from a new perspective and upside down they put things right.